PRESENTED TO

_____

FROM

_____

DATE

_____

COACH FOR LIFE

Other Books by Jim Stovall

The Ultimate Gift

The Ultimate Life

The Ultimate Journey

The Ultimate Legacy

The Ultimate Financial Plan

Ultimate Hindsight

Ultimate Productivity

The Gift of a Legacy

A Christmas Snow

The Millionaire Map

Millionaire Answers

The Lamp

Today's the Day!

Success Secrets of Super Achievers

The Art of Learning and Self-Development

The Art of Productivity

The Art of Presentation

The Art of Communication

The Art of Entrepreneurship

The Financial Crossroads

Keeper of the Flame

100 Worst Employees

The Will to Win

Wisdom of the Ages

Discovering Joye

Top of the Hill

One Season of Hope

Wisdom for Winners Volumes 1, 2, 3, 4

Poems, Quotes, and Things to Think About

Passport to Success (with Dr. Greg Reid)

Words That Shaped Our World 1 (with Kathy Johnson)

Words That Shaped Our World 2 (with Kathy Johnson)

COACH FOR LIFE

A Parable of Learning
How to Play the Game,
Live Your Life,
and Win

JIM STOVALL

© Copyright 2025– Jim Stovall

All rights reserved. This book is protected by the copyright laws of the United States of America. No part of this publication may be reproduced, stored in or introduced into a retrieval system, or transmitted, in any form or by any means (electronic, mechanical, photocopying, recording or otherwise), without the prior written permission of the publisher. For permissions requests, contact the publisher, addressed "Attention: Permissions Coordinator," at the address below.

Published and distributed by:
SOUND WISDOM
P.O. Box 310
Shippensburg, PA 17257-0310

717-530-2122

info@soundwisdom.com

www.soundwisdom.com

While efforts have been made to verify information contained in this publication, neither the author nor the publisher assumes any responsibility for errors, inaccuracies, or omissions. While this publication is chock-full of useful, practical information; it is not intended to be legal or accounting advice. All readers are advised to seek competent lawyers and accountants to follow laws and regulations that may apply to specific situations. The reader of this publication assumes responsibility for the use of the information. The author and publisher assume no responsibility or liability whatsoever on the behalf of the reader of this publication.

The scanning, uploading and distribution of this publication via the Internet or via any other means without the permission of the publisher is illegal and punishable by law. Please purchase only authorized editions and do not participate in or encourage piracy of copyrightable materials.

ISBN 13 TP: 978-1-64095-606-3

ISBN 13 eBook: 978-1-64095-607-0

For Worldwide Distribution, Printed in the U.S.A.

1 2025

Dedication

This book is dedicated to the many coaches in my athletic, academic, business, and personal life. You have all left your mark and made a difference.

Contents

1   Winning Through Reading 15

"The key to anything you want to be, do, or have is within the pages of a book."

2   Winning Through Collaboration. 23

"When you're working with the right people, one plus one equals ten."

3   Winning Through Time. 31

"The worst thing you can be is a thief, and the worst thing you can steal is time."

4   Winning Through Ownership 41

"You can be forgiven for making a mistake but not for making excuses."

5   Winning Through Money 49

"Money is one of the least important elements of life, but it impacts all of the most important elements."

6   Winning Through Learning 57
"Learning is a race we run that never ends."

7   Winning Through Overcoming 67
*"Excellence becomes possible when we get
over the notion that life is fair."*

8   Winning Through Urgency.........................75
*"In the world of success, there's no such
thing as someday. Today's the day."*

9   Winning Through Belief 83
"Our achievements are only limited by our beliefs."

10   Winning Through Integrity........................91
"All success begins and ends with keeping your word."

11   Winning Through Effort 99
*"When you think you've done your best and have no more
to give, you will find there is still more in your tank."*

12   Winning Through Relationships 107
*"The most important things in our lives are
the relationships we have with others."*

13   Winning Through Giving 115
*"The most rewarding thing you can do with
your time, effort, or money is give it away."*

14 Winning Through Understanding 123

"Virtually all questions and conflicts relating to the human condition can be resolved through the Golden Rule."

15 Winning Through Priorities 131

"Excellence is only required at a few critical moments. Unfortunately, we never know when they're coming."

16 Winning Through Planning 139

"Effort without planning is chaos."

17 Winning Through Leadership 147

"If you want to be a leader, learn how to serve."

18 Winning Through Consistency 153

"Turn your best performance into a habit."

19 Winning Through Laughter 161

"If you can't laugh at yourself, the whole world will be laughing at you."

20 Winning Through Gratitude 169

"The quickest way to get what you want is to be thankful for what you already have."

21 Winning Through Legacy 177

"The most important seeds we plant will bloom long after we're gone."

About Jim Stovall 185

1

Winning Through Reading

"The key to anything you want to be, do, or have is within the pages of a book."
—Coach Mason G. Edwards

My dear reader, you and I are preparing to take a journey within the pages of this novel. Beginning in the next chapter, we will be transported to a different time and place and be introduced to some compelling characters. While the setting and plot are fictional, and the characters are figments of my imagination, I can assure you the life lessons and powerful principles you will be exposed to are among the most significant and valuable I have ever written.

You are currently undertaking one of the activities that is part of the majority of successful people's lives. In surveys of self-made millionaires, top CEOs, and successful entrepreneurs, it was found that one of the few traits they share in common involves regularly reading motivational and inspirational books.

Early in our education, we learn to read, which enables us to spend the rest of our lives reading to learn. As the author of more than 50 books, nine of which have been turned into movies—which I believe will be the case with this story—I am often reminded of the time in my life when reading played virtually no role in my world.

When I could read with my eyes as you are reading the print on a page or characters on a digital screen right now, I don't know that I ever read an entire book cover to cover. After losing my sight and learning to live as a blind person, I participated in a national study conducted by the US Department of Education to determine how fast people could listen to compressed digital audio books and retain the material. When the study was concluded, I continued on my own to the point where over the past 30 years, thanks to this high-speed technology, I have been able to literally read a book every day. Becoming a reader made me want to be a writer, and it has opened new worlds, powerful thoughts, and unique ideas to me that have created previously unimagined success in every area of my life.

One of my late, great movie partners, Scott Fithian, often said, "If you can tell a great story, you earn the right to share your message." You may have noticed among the very first pages in this book is a presentation page that allows you to gift this book to loved ones, friends, or colleagues. When we learn something, we change our own lives. When we teach it, we change other people's lives—but when we teach people to teach, we can literally change the world. As you take this journey with me, I hope you will be thinking of those people in your world whom you would like to join us in this quest.

As a young man, I had only one ambition in life which was to be an All-American football player and then make my living in the NFL. The scouts and coaches that monitor such things assured me I had the size, speed, and talent to live out my dream. During a routine physical before beginning fall practice one year, I was diagnosed with the condition that would cause me to lose my sight. Realizing that my football career had ended, I was exposed to Olympic weightlifting and, as my sight declined, was able to complete my athletic career as a National Olympic weightlifting champion.

My father had played Minor League baseball as a young man, and my brother was a very talented basketball player. Sports were an important element of our home as I was growing up. In *Coach for Life,* you are going to meet Mason G. Edwards through the eyes and lives of those he touched on the football field, baseball diamond, and basketball court.

As an athlete, I was exposed to many coaches, and all of them left their fingerprints on my life. Now as a speaker, author, movie producer, columnist, and radio commentator, I've been exposed to a number of life coaches whose work extends beyond the athletic arena. Sports make a great vehicle for life lessons. Success or failure, as well as winning or losing, are compressed into an extremely finite and digestible time and place. Few of us will ever make our living playing the sports we love, but we can be forever elevated by the lessons they offer us.

As a young child, there were two towering sports figures that my father exposed me to via the television broadcasts of their exploits. While we would often catch random games or sporting events, we never missed watching legendary Coach John Wooden who led his UCLA Bruins to ten national basketball championships in twelve years—a feat that will likely never be equaled. We also never missed the incomparable golfer Jack Nicklaus who won more major championships than anyone who has ever played that venerable sport. My father explained to me that both Coach Wooden and Mr. Nicklaus were people whose examples I should follow both in competition and, more importantly, in life.

It is an irony and a blessing that I got to meet and befriend both Jack Nicklaus and John Wooden as a result of them reading my books and contacting me. I will never forget the day I was sitting in my office, which is decorated with sports memorabilia including several things from Jack Nicklaus and John Wooden, when the young lady at the front desk excitedly ran into my office proclaiming, "John Wooden is on the phone and wants to talk with you."

While I appreciated her enthusiasm, as she was fully aware of my admiration for Coach Wooden, I let her down gently responding, "There must be thousands of guys named John Wooden, and since I have millions of books in print that have our contact information, it's inevitable that someone named John Wooden might call." She remained resolute and let me know that while there may be many John Wooden's in the world, there's probably only one who wanted me to autograph a number of books for him including one made out to Kareem Abdul-Jabbar.

That call was the genesis of a number of telephone conversations that took place between Coach Wooden and me from the time he was 95 years old until we lost him just before his 100th birthday.

In much the same way, the mayor of my city gave one of my novels to Jack Nicklaus, and he became a fan and friend, while I continue to see him as a mentor and the living embodiment of so many of the lessons my father wanted to pass on to me.

As someone who has lived the past three decades of my life without sight, I retain some powerful visual images that I can call up whenever I need to revisit them. One of these priceless pictures is Jack Nicklaus poised over a difficult putt he needed to make to win the Masters. The television camera was across the green, so as Mr. Nicklaus read the green and prepared to putt, he was staring directly into the camera lens and onto our television screen. That level of focus, intensity, and determination is something few people ever experience.

Mr. Nicklaus told me years later that he never hit a golf shot until he had already seen it in his mind successfully executed. He made that putt and went on to win his sixth Masters, becoming the oldest man at that time to ever win that prestigious tournament.

The visual image I will always have of Coach John Wooden is of him placidly sitting on the end of the bench watching his team perform on the court. He was dressed impeccably in a conservative suit and tie and always held a rolled-up program. During an era when many coaches would scream, get red in the face, and throw things on the court including chairs, John Wooden looked as if he was preparing to take a nap. Later, he told me that the people we lead will always take their cues from us. *"If my players see me serene and confident, they will play up to their potential knowing that they are in total control of the contest."*

Coach Wooden left me with two phrases that empower my life. When things are difficult or challenging, I always recall him saying, *"Things turn out best for those who make the best of the way things turn out."* And the most impactful thought I ever got from Coach Wooden represents his legacy to me which remains his challenge, *"Before you attempt to do anything big or small, ask yourself the simple question, what would I do right now if I were amazing?"* That simple phrase reminds us that everything in life is important, and we always have the opportunity to be amazing.

While they won't be directly credited, the influence of both Coach Wooden and Jack Nicklaus is powerful and prominent within these pages. I believe it is fitting that they each have learning institutions named after them. In California, you will find John Wooden High School, and in Florida you can visit the Jack Nicklaus Academy. Learning lessons in competitions and not carrying them into your personal and professional life is a waste of a precious natural resource.

I am honored that you invested the time, money, and effort to take this trip with me. If you proceed with an open mind and a willing heart, I'm convinced that you will be forever changed.

—Jim Stovall, 2025

2

Winning Through Collaboration

"When you're working with the right people, one plus one equals ten."
—Coach Mason G. Edwards

COACH FOR LIFE

The distant glow in the sky that could be seen for miles around was a familiar and ever-present fixture throughout the fall in little towns all across the country. That familiar glow is known far and wide as Friday Night Lights and signals a home football game that represents a fierce competition, community event, and cultural experience. On that particular evening however, it wasn't Friday night, and the calendar showed that it was spring, not fall. The football stadium was to serve as the venue for a very different and even more significant event.

The memorial tribute for Coach Mason G. Edwards was both an occasion for mourning the loss of an irreplaceable icon and the opportunity to celebrate the life of a powerful individual who impacted everyone around him. I had met the coach more than 50 years earlier when he came into my office looking for a job.

My name is Gill Lucas, and throughout my working life, I was the athletic director at Riverview High School. After I reached mandatory retirement age, I become a volunteer assistant and team manager for Coach Edwards. But when I first hired him, the only qualifications he had that were readily apparent to me were that he was very young, extremely energetic, and willing to coach football, basketball, and baseball for the meager salary I had to offer. When our brief interview ended with a handshake signaling his acceptance of the job and my welcoming him to Riverview High School, little did

I know that I had just encountered the most influential and impactful person in my life.

While the school board had adhered rigidly to the mandatory retirement age when I had my 65th birthday, no one had the nerve or audacity to mention it when Coach Edwards was approaching 80. He had been struggling with all the inevitable ailments that come with aging, but it never seemed to affect him when he confronted his players. That frail old man could turn into a towering giant when the whistle blew and it was time for him to fulfill his role as the coach. He was like Mount Rushmore or the Grand Canyon as he seemed permanent and indestructible.

No one who had ever encountered Coach Edwards could fathom the world without him. Then came that fateful day when I got the call from his wife Margaret, who had been by his side at the hospital, informing me that he was gone. I knew I would have to grieve and come to terms with my loss, but first and foremost, I had to accept the reality that my friend and colleague, Coach Mason G. Edwards, had died.

We were right in the middle of baseball season and juggling spring football at the same time when all my focus and energy, along with that of the whole town, was directed toward the memorial service and tribute for Coach Edwards. The only possible venue to hold such an event in our little town was the football stadium, so the word went out far and wide to those who had been touched and transformed throughout Coach Edwards' half-century of shaping athletes and high-quality people. Once all the arrangements were made and the memorial event was organized, I was left with my grief and an unfathomable void in my life. Although my friend and colleague was gone, his words, example, and influence had become a permanent part of my mind and soul.

As I drove toward the stadium, through the middle of the modest business district of Riverview, there was an eerie silence, and there were no other cars on the streets nor pedestrians on the sidewalks. I reached over to the passenger's seat and grabbed the clipboard that held a lengthy to-do list of tasks I needed to accomplish before the memorial service began. I had delivered my obligatory statements to the media, picked up several VIPs at our regional airport, and checked off each of the other items on my list. I consulted my watch and confirmed that I had just enough time to make it to the stadium and change into my funeral suit, which I had left in my office under the stadium. Being late was never an option but certainly not on that day.

I was still a mile from the stadium when I noticed cars parked on both sides of the road as far as my eyes could see. In my 50 years of experience at many games and events in that stadium, I had never seen a crowd like the one that was gathering for the farewell memorial service for my colleague and friend. Thankfully, as the former athletic director and now volunteer team manager, I had a key that would permit me to open the gate to the small lot where the buses parked to pick up and drop off teams outside of the locker room.

I parked my car and bounded up the steps as quickly as a person who has lived almost eight decades can do when I was stopped in my tracks by a sign on the locker room door. I know I had seen that sign thousands of times before, but at that particular moment, it took on a deeper meaning and more significance.

The sign proclaimed, "WARNING: Anyone entering here immediately ceases to be an individual and becomes part of a team." It was signed: Coach Mason G. Edwards. That sign gave me both a sense of pride and responsibility as I walked through the locker room and rushed toward my closet of an office. Before I reached my destination, I passed the open door of Coach Edwards' inner sanctum. I paused and observed a scene I had confronted countless times, but was somehow now seeing for the first time.

Hanging behind his desk was a curious sight that I had become accustomed to seeing many times each day for decades. Shortly after I hired the young Coach Mason G. Edwards, I heard pounding in his office and found him nailing a fork and spoon to the wall behind his desk. They were like any normal utensils except for the fact that they had three-foot long handles. The coach placed them behind his desk chair like crossed swords. When I asked him about them, he shared with me an ancient parable that seemed somehow familiar but at the same time it challenged everything I had believed about the concept of a team.

The young coach sat on the edge of his desk and described two similar but completely opposite visions. The verbal scenes he painted for me were those of Heaven and hell. In both scenes, a group of people were gathered around a table with a sumptuous banquet laid out before them. In hell, the people were sad, depressed, and starving because their three-foot long forks and spoons made it impossible for them to feed themselves. In a similar view of Heaven, the people were gratefully and eagerly enjoying the feast as they happily fed one another with the extended silverware.

That imagery was seared into the minds of everyone who ever confronted Coach Mason G. Edwards. He often quoted an author he had admired and later befriended, named Zig Ziglar who said, "You can have anything in life you want if you'll help enough other people get what they want."

Next to the unforgettable fork and spoon hung an old black and white framed photo of Coach Edwards in his youth wearing a basketball uniform and standing next to a teammate, but the two of them were polar opposites. The grainy picture revealed young Mason Edwards to be pale and undersized, and, though he told me the photo was taken when he was 15 and a member of the All-State freshman basketball team, he looked about 12. His teammate was powerfully built and towered at least a foot over young Mason. I would have described him as an African American college student as he looked like he had passed his fifteenth birthday at least five years earlier.

I will never forget Coach Edwards describing their experience that summer. "After we made the All-Star team, we got to travel and play freshman All-Star teams from other states. It was a big deal for my best friend Clete and me. It was a different time and place, and I'll never forget when our school bus rolled into a hot, humid, sleepy little town somewhere in the south. We all stumbled off the bus and our coach led us into the lobby of a cheap motel where we would stay until the game the following night.

Clete and I were standing next to one another. In those years, we were never far apart and were roommates on the road. The motel manager nodded to our coach and let him know that all our rooms were ready, but then he frowned and pointed toward Clete as he informed everyone that he couldn't stay there. We all stood in stunned silence as, even in those days, athletic teams were totally color blind.

I believe it was in that next moment when I started thinking about and moving toward my future profession when I heard our coach inform the team and the motel manager that we travel together, we play together, and we stay together. We left immediately, and our entire team spent a cramped but unforgettable night of comradery sleeping on the bus. We wouldn't have traded it for a five-star hotel because "we were a team."

I rushed into my office, threw on my somber blue suit, and paused briefly before walking into the stadium. I felt uncomfortable, inadequate, and unprepared, but I did what I knew Coach Edwards would want me to do because I was part of the team.

3

Winning Through Time

"The worst thing you can be is a thief, and the worst thing you can steal is time."
—Coach Mason G. Edwards

The venerable, old Riverview Pioneers stadium had never seen a crowd like the one assembled that day. The bleachers were filled to overflowing, and folding chairs had been lined up the entire length and breadth of the field. As I climbed the stairs up to the giant platform that had been erected in the north end zone, I glimpsed the two Jumbotron screens above the stage that were showing highlights of Coach Edwards' career. Generations of football, basketball, and baseball players performed with skill and enthusiasm just as they had been taught.

It was my job to open the program by welcoming everyone and introducing Spencer Rollins. As I glanced at those seated behind the podium who were slated to speak, I noticed Spencer Rollins was front and center. He smiled, glanced at his watch, and gave me a thumbs up.

I stood at the podium and marveled at the immense crowd that had gathered to say thank you and goodbye to Coach Mason G. Edwards. I took a deep breath, cleared my throat, and began.

"Thank you all for coming. I am Gill Lucas former athletic director, current volunteer manager, and forever a proud member of Coach Edwards' team.

"For those of you who knew the Coach, there's nothing I really need to say. And for anyone who didn't know the Coach, there's really nothing I can say. On occasions such as this, it is customary to speak of someone's accomplishments, but today

Mason Edwards' accomplishments are here to speak for themselves." Heads nodded and there was a brief round of applause.

"Now the task falls to me to introduce Spencer Rollins. I will keep this introduction very brief, not because Spencer isn't worthy of a lengthy introduction, but the fact is, anywhere in the country, Spencer Rollins simply needs no introduction. So please join me in welcoming an All-American, a member of the Pro-Football Hall of Fame, and the popular host of Monday Night Football, a lifelong Riverview Pioneer, Spencer Rollins."

The crowd rose to their feet and a thunderous ovation echoed through the stadium. Spencer stood at the podium like a chiseled heroic ebony statue. He glanced at the gold watch on his wrist again and smiled as he began, "Please let the record show that on this momentous day, we got started right on time. As you observed when you entered the stadium, the highlights of Coach's career were already playing because as Coach always said..."

The entire crowd responded in unison, "If you're not ten minutes early, you're late."

Spencer nodded in satisfaction and admitted, "I didn't always know that and unfortunately, I had to learn it the hard way."

Spencer Rollins paused and gazed over the enormous crowd. Everyone gathered there had their own private thoughts and memories of him. Virtually everyone in Riverview had seen him on Monday Night Football. The giant billboard at the edge of our town proclaimed, "Home of Spencer Rollins a Legendary Riverview Pioneer."

Some in the crowd were old enough to have seen him playing in the NFL for over a decade—a career which culminated in Spencer Rollins being inducted into the Pro Football Hall of Fame. A few of us who were gathered there in the stadium remembered him setting records that still stand at our state university, and the eldest among us remembered watching him play on the same field where we were assembled that special evening.

Spencer paused and his voice and manner took us all back in time. He began, "I grew up in Riverview. Many of the experiences I appreciate today seemed to be hardships at the time. I never really knew my father as he wasn't around much. My mom was working all the time to try to keep our family afloat. All of us kids were pretty much responsible for taking care of ourselves, and I didn't do a very good job of managing me.

"On the opening day of practice during my freshman year, I walked into this stadium for the first time. I didn't have a dad, I didn't have any discipline, and I didn't have a direction for my life. Little did I know, I would find all three on this football field."

Spencer Rollins pointed to the field that was now covered with thousands of people sitting in folding chairs. He shared his memories of arriving after practice had already begun on that first day. He wasn't sure what he was expected to do, so he approached the man wearing a whistle around his neck and holding a clipboard.

He explained, "I stood about six feet away from Coach Edwards, and I could tell he was aware that I was there, but he wouldn't even acknowledge me. Finally, when there was break in the action on the field, he just turned and stared at me."

Spencer allowed a long pause to stretch out, and he demonstrated his version of the Coach Mason G. Edwards stare that became both familiar and dreaded by a half-century of athletes at Riverview High School. Spencer recounted his memory of Coach glaring at him and finally asking, "Who are you and what do you want?"

Spencer remembered that he had just given the coach that teenage shrug, and Coach Edwards pointed to the bench and ordered, "Sit over there until you figure it out."

Spencer Rollins remembered, "I sat there for two hours and missed the entire first practice. When the coach blew his whistle signaling the end of practice, and the team jogged toward the locker room, I followed a few paces behind the coach. When he got to the locker room door, he turned to me and announced, "Practice is at 9 a.m. tomorrow, and if you're not ten minutes early, you're late."

Spencer chuckled recalling, "Then he slammed the door in my face."

Laughter echoed throughout the stadium as Spencer continued. "Well, the next day, I was there ten minutes early, and my life changed when the coach let me run one play on the first team offense, and we were going up against the first team defense. The only direction he gave me was to line up behind the quarterback and don't move until the ball is snapped. Then, he'll pitch it to you and see if you can get around the corner and down the sideline before that all-state defensive end takes your head off." Everyone listened with rapt attention at Spencer's memories of that long ago scene.

He continued, "I don't know whether it was fear, frustration, or just finding my purpose in life, but I caught the ball, made it to the corner a step before the defensive end, and ran down the entire sideline into the end zone. I thought Coach Edwards would be ecstatic or at least pleased, but he just noncommittally nodded his head and signaled for me to sit on the bench."

Spencer's memories flowed out of him, and he recounted play after play in those pre-season fall practices when a lowly freshman ran past, through, or over the best defenders on the team. He recalled, "I was pretty sure a superstar had been born until Coach posted the starting lineup the week of our first game. I couldn't find my name on the first team, so I flipped the page and looked at the second team, but I wasn't there either. Finally, I found my name on the bottom of the third page simply listed as a reserve player at my position. I summoned all my courage, walked down that long hall past the locker room, and knocked on the coach's door."

Spencer rapped his knuckles on the podium, so that the sound was picked up by the microphone and heard throughout the stadium. He recalled, "The coach asked me in and told me to sit down.

"When I asked why I wasn't the starting running back, the coach leaned back in his chair, took a deep breath, and shared with me the wisdom that changed my career and my life."

Spencer paused then recited Coach Edwards' words, "Spencer, you're not a good football player. You are a great football player, and maybe the best one I've ever seen, but you're useless if you're not in place and ready to go when we need you. Being late is never acceptable. It tells your teammates that you don't care, and they are not important to you."

Spencer became emotional as he explained how Coach Mason G. Edwards had given him the facts of life. He reminisced, "Coach told me that time is the most precious commodity we have. It can never be replaced or restored. He explained football is a game of inches, but it is played by the second. If you have only one second left, you can run a play and win the game. But if you're not ready and time runs out, you lose. The coach gave me a graduate course letting me know that procrastination is being late for a commitment to yourself, and his concept of pre-crastination, or getting something done beforehand, is like being ten minutes early for an appointment with yourself."

Spencer smiled and nodded as he admitted, "If you check the record books for my freshman season, you will see that I broke the school and conference rushing record. But what you won't see in those record books is the fact that I didn't start one game that year. Coach put another player into the game for the first series and brought me in off the bench. He showed me through his words and deeds that time, indeed, waits for no man regardless of how well you can run with a football."

The crowd smiled and laughed as they nodded their understanding.

Spencer seemed to transform from that 15-year-old freshman back into the superstar and media icon we all knew. He concluded, "I got my first job on television because I was sitting in the chair in front of the camera ten minutes before the appointment. And you can rest assured, when you see me on Monday Night Football, I was there ready to go before the lights came on and the camera rolled. Many great things have happened to me in my life, but they all began in this place with a coach who cared enough to teach me how to respect myself and everyone around me by being on time every time."

Spencer Rollins stepped back from the podium and turned as the crowd exploded into thunderous applause. I had known him as his athletic director and enjoyed him for many years as a fan. But in that moment, I hugged Spencer Rollins as a true friend.

As the applause died down, Spencer returned to his seat on the stage, and I consulted my agenda as I prepared to introduce the next speaker who would honor my colleague and lifelong friend, Coach Mason G. Edwards.

4

Winning Through Ownership

"You can be forgiven for making a mistake but not for making excuses."
—Coach Mason G. Edwards

The familiar confines of the Riverview Pioneers football stadium had somehow changed and shifted. For over half a century in my career as athletic director and then in my voluntary role as athletic manager, I felt my job was to be available to support and assist my colleague and friend Mason Edwards. In every situation, I would always locate him in any setting and be available at a moment's notice to step in as needed.

On the night of his memorial service in the packed football stadium, I realized he was not there, but he seemed to be everywhere. Many of the tasks I had performed throughout the decades were thankless jobs that went unnoticed by everyone except Coach Edwards. He never took anything for granted and always reminded me that the details make the difference.

Speaking before a small gathering made me uncomfortable. I would have felt inadequate to address the thousands of people assembled except I was there to remember and honor my lifelong colleague and friend. It just seemed to flow naturally as I began, "Ladies and gentlemen, as someone who spent much of my working life loading athletic equipment and picking up wet towels from the locker room floor, introducing the governor of our state is not something that comes naturally to me especially after his dramatic arrival in a helicopter that landed on our baseball field on the other side of the school ten minutes before we started this memorial service."

The crowd laughed at the irony of the situation. I was pleased to see that the governor was smiling so I continued, "Everyone knows him as the honorable governor of our state, but some of us remember him as an outstanding student and a pretty fair power forward on our Riverview Pioneers basketball team. So please welcome one of our own, Governor Curtis Sutton." The crowd rose to their feet as one and welcomed the governor with a thunderous and prolonged ovation.

He waved at the crowd and as the applause faded out, he began, "In spite of your overwhelming welcome, I'm reminded that my campaign pollsters told me that at least forty percent of you didn't vote for me." The laughter seemed to make the governor more human and just another one of the many people who had been impacted by Coach Edwards. It was obvious the governor had a lot of experience speaking to crowds. "I want to thank my friend and former Athletic Director Gill Lucas for that wonderful introduction, but describing me as a power forward may be a bit of an exaggeration. I did, indeed, play forward and on a couple of occasions might have demonstrated minimal power."

The governor settled in as he shared his memories, and the crowd seemed to be caught up in the moment. "I am proud to be governor of this great state, but I am more proud to say that I am a Riverview Pioneer who counted Coach Mason G. Edwards among my friends." The crowd applauded enthusiastically as Curtis Sutton seemed to transition from one of the most powerful political leaders in the country back into an insecure adolescent.

"My journey to the governor's mansion began in this place. The lessons I learned here from Coach lead and guide me every day. I remember during my junior year, due to an injury to one of our best players, I started in a conference championship game. With four seconds to go, we were behind by one point, and we had the ball. Coach Edwards called a time-out and diagramed a play in which I would take the final shot from the corner. The play unfolded on the court just as he had diagramed it, but at the critical moment, I missed the shot. Thankfully, my teammate and lifelong friend, Brian Klemmer, tipped it in at the buzzer."

The governor gazed into the crowd and asked, "Where is Brian Klemmer?" A man in the bleachers stood. The governor chuckled and continued, "As you can see, Klemmer might be five-foot-eight on a good day, and when he tipped that ball in for the win, he went over the top of their All-State center who had to be at least six-foot-eight." The crowd cheered as if the Pioneers had just won the game.

The governor continued. "I was distraught that I had failed. When the coach patted me on the back, I let him know I was sorry I had missed the shot and let everyone down, but I was grateful Brian tipped it in and erased my mistake." Curtis Sutton glared at the audience as if he were the coach, then he repeated Coach Edwards long-ago words, "We win as a team and we lose as a team. There are no exceptions to that rule. You didn't miss a shot, and Klemmer didn't tip it in. *We* missed the shot, and *we* tipped it in and won the game. Any single play during that entire game by any player on the floor could have changed the one-point outcome. Always remember you can accomplish anything if you don't care who gets the credit, and you can solve any problem if you don't care who gets the blame." The crowd applauded and nodded as they had all heard the coach share those thoughts countless times.

The governor continued, "We politicians at the state capitol and those in Washington could learn a lot from the coach's wisdom about taking credit and projecting blame." The governor reached inside his jacket and withdrew a leather wallet. He said, "A life in public service provides many mementos and treasured keepsakes, but none more precious than this one. I am never without it."

The governor lovingly opened the leather wallet and withdrew a worn letter. He carefully unfolded it and began to read. "Curtis/Governor, I want to congratulate you on your victory today and on becoming the governor of our state. Always remember that governors and coaches work for those they serve. They lead by example, and their only legacy is creating value in the lives of others. You can never control tomorrow until you take full responsibility for yesterday and today.

"As you lead those at the state capitol, be mindful of what I learned as a coach. Whenever possible, try to catch people doing something right, and don't forget some players need a pat on the back, while others require a pat a little lower and a little harder." Laughter interrupted the governor. He smiled, then as the stadium fell silent, he continued reading.

"A leader is a leader all the time. You don't get a day off. You will be known for a lifetime of great service or one moral lapse or failure in judgment. We all want to be liked by those we serve, but it is more important that we are always respected. People may disagree with your decisions, but never let them question your integrity. You will be in my thoughts and prayers as you fulfill this important role and serve all the people of our state." The governor wiped a tear from his eye and concluded the reading, "It is signed: Proudly and Respectfully, Coach Mason G. Edwards."

The governor carefully refolded the letter, slid it back into the leather wallet and returned the wallet to his pocket. Curtis Sutton resumed his governor's demeanor and spoke. "Well, our friend and beloved coach is gone, but he will never be forgotten. And in a very special way, he will always be with us. Those who have left a legacy behind never fade away. Each of us takes Coach Edwards' words and deeds into our world every day. Whether you're a businessperson, a laborer, a teacher, member of the clergy, or those filling the most important role in our world as parents, Coach Edwards has made us all who we are, and as we follow his example, through us, he will impact and make his mark on the next generation."

The governor looked to his right and held out his hand. An alert member of his security team stepped forward and placed a document in his hand. Governor Sutton proclaimed, "As the governor of this state, I make the following proclamation. Whereas Coach Mason G. Edwards for more than half a century guided and led the young people of Riverview through their various sports competitions and into their adult lives; and whereas beyond the coach's unprecedented winning records and professional accomplishments, he made our state and the world a better place; and whereas his legacy has become a fixture within Riverview and across the entire state, I proclaim that going forward on this date each year, we will celebrate and recognize Coach Mason G. Edwards Day throughout the state."

The crowd rose to their feet in a thunderous standing ovation. The governor handed me the proclamation, patted me on the back, and said, "Gill, thank you for letting me be part of this." The governor was surrounded by his security detail as he left the stage. As the applause continued, I held the official proclamation over my head for all to see.

5

Winning Through Money

"Money is one of the least important elements of life, but it impacts all of the most important elements."
—Coach Mason G. Edwards

There was a myriad of emotions in the Riverview football stadium that spring evening. Many people had their heads bowed or were openly weeping as if they were at a graveside funeral service, while others seemed to be at an enthusiastic pep rally honoring the memory of their beloved Coach Mason G. Edwards. The gravity and importance of the occasion was punctuated as we could all hear the governor's helicopter taking off and fading into the distance. I once again stood at the podium and spoke.

"As Coach Edwards' sometimes boss, sometimes assistant, and forevermore friend and colleague, I spent countless hours over many days and years discussing student athletes here in Riverview. I can honestly say Coach loved each of you and was concerned for you all, but he rarely talked about you as athletes. He realized that, with a few exceptions like Spencer Rollins, most of you would apply the lessons you learned on the football field, basketball court, or baseball diamond elsewhere in life.

"Now I want to introduce you to someone we all know and admire. Jay Henderson has taken the lessons he learned as an athlete, and he has applied them in the marketplace creating much success that has resulted in many job opportunities and untold philanthropy that is truly making a difference far and wide. Please welcome corporate CEO, industrialist, developer, and generous benefactor, Jay Henderson."

The crowd applauded vigorously. Most of them knew Jay by reputation if not personally. He is one of those successful people whose wealth does not invoke envy but creates a sense of hope and possibility in everyone. Jay Henderson strode confidently to the podium in a suit that may have cost more than my car. He smiled warmly and then, in a down-to-earth manner, began to speak.

"It is truly an honor and a privilege to be here today because were it not for Coach Edwards, nothing you have ever heard about me would have happened, and my life would have been quite different." Jay paused and I could almost see him going back, in his mind, to a very different time and place. He sighed and recounted a piece of his life.

"I was born here in Riverview, or at least I assume I was. All I know about my family background and birth is that I was discovered on the steps of the fire station when I was about three hours old. I have never learned anything about my family to this very day. I grew up in a series of orphanages, group homes, and with an endless string of foster families. The first consistency or structure I had in my life was when I signed up to play for the coach. I needed a mentor and father figure so badly that I played football, basketball, *and* baseball for him. I would have competed in darts and checkers if we had a team."

The crowd laughed and settled in eagerly as Jay's story continued to unfold. "I was walking to the orphanage where I had been staying while I was hoping someone would adopt me. It was hot that summer day after football practice, and the dirt road was uphill and dusty. I think when you're at a bad place in your life, all roads are hot, uphill, and dusty." Some of the crowd laughed while others nodded as if they had experienced their own tough roads.

Jay explained, "Most of my teammates had bicycles, motorcycles, or even cars, but everything I owned in those days would fit in one trash bag with room left over. A couple of my teammates had offered me a ride, but I was too embarrassed to have them drop me off at the orphanage." Jay Henderson took a deep breath as he struggled with the weight of his memories, then he seemed to turn a hopeful corner as he continued.

"Then, that fancy pickup truck many of you will remember pulled up beside me. The passenger window rolled down, and Coach told me to get in. In those days and for the rest of his life, when Coach told me to get in, I got in." The crowd reacted enthusiastically, understanding the impact of Coach Mason G. Edwards.

Jay picked up where he had left off in his account of that fateful day. "Coach didn't ask where I was going or how to get there. He just started driving toward the orphanage. I commented sarcastically about rich people who drive fancy trucks. He slammed on his brakes, and we stopped right in the middle of the road. I could take you back to that very spot today even though it's been almost forty years. The coach asked me what I knew about people who were financially successful, and I told him they were either very lucky or they lied, cheated, and stole.

"The coach turned his truck around and drove into a neighborhood of huge homes. They looked like palaces with manicured lawns and gardens. He pulled into one of the driveways and began speaking to me with that attitude and tone we all came to know and love."

Jay Henderson paused and glanced to his right as if he were the coach looking at someone in the passenger's seat. He recited Mason Edwards' words as if the coach were speaking himself, "Son, since you know so much about people's financial history, motivation, and character from seeing their vehicles or houses, what would you say about the people who live here?" Jay let an uncomfortable pause linger, then spoke.

"I had no idea what he expected me to say, so I just blurted out my thoughts explaining that whoever lived there had taken advantage of poor, less fortunate people, and they ought to be willing to share some of what they were lucky enough to get. As the coach backed out of the driveway, he told me that the Sullivan family lived in that house, and Marvin Sullivan was a friend of his. He went on to explain that Mr. Sullivan grew up in the same orphanage where I was living. The coach drove for a few minutes then stopped in front of the brand-new community center, which at that time was the pride and joy of Riverview. The coach pointed at the sign and told me to read it."

Jay stood at the podium and the crowd could sense his discomfort those decades ago. He answered somewhat timidly as if he were speaking to the coach, "The sign says Sullivan

Community Center. We left there and visited the Sullivan Library and the new Sullivan wing of our Riverview Hospital. I asked the coach why rich people always want to put their name on everything they do. Coach responded in that tone that always lets you know he thinks you have the intelligence of a tree stump." The crowd exploded with laughter and several elbowed one another obviously recalling when the coach had confronted them the same way.

When the stadium fell silent again, Jay Henderson spoke as the confident executive and multimillionaire businessman he had become, "Coach informed me in no uncertain terms that he knew for a fact Mr. Sullivan gave a lot of money to things anonymously but, with some of his projects, he wanted to put his name on them so that someday another orphan like me could see the example and begin to explore the possibilities.

"Then Coach Edwards gave me his pregame locker room talk for financial success. He told me there was nothing shameful about being in poverty as long as I didn't let the poverty be in me. He told me that becoming wealthy is not selfish because the only way to get money is to create value in the lives of other people. He told me that even though teachers and coaches don't make much money, they are the fastest growing group of new millionaires because you can make your money work as hard for you as you work for it. Then Coach Edwards gave me the challenge of my life when he let me know success is not only about going from poverty to prosperity, but instead, it's about going from poverty to prosperity to purpose. The coach handed me a card and told me to keep it with me."

Jay Henderson reached into his pocket and withdrew a card that had worn and yellowed with age. He read it aloud, "You make a living from what you get, but you make a life from what you give. Signed, Winston Churchill." The entire stadium fell silent. You could have heard a pin drop as we all knew we had heard a profound and transformational message.

Jay Henderson announced, "Before I get off the stage so you can hear from some *really* wonderful people, I want to introduce you to the first ten recipients of the annual Coach Mason G. Edwards College Scholarship funded by the Henderson Foundation."

The crowd stood and cheered as ten bright, young seniors at Riverview High School paraded across the stage. Jay Henderson beamed with pride and concluded, "Ladies and gentlemen, many years ago, I stopped calculating my wealth based on how much money I had and began calculating my wealth based upon the caliber and quality of my friends. I can assure you I am a wealthy man because I can honestly say Coach Mason G. Edwards was my friend."

Jay Henderson waved to the crowd, shook my hand, and gave me a priceless gift when he said, "I would have never been here without him, and he would have never been here without you."

6

Winning Through Learning

"Learning is a race we run that never ends."
—Coach Mason G. Edwards

Jay Henderson's expression of gratitude caused a lump in my throat that I was afraid might keep me from being able to make my next introduction. As I looked across the stadium at the overwhelming crowd that had come to pay tribute to a coach and friend, I was struck by the fact that I could have never done what Mason Edwards did, but as his colleague and part of the team, I shared in his victory.

I glanced at the next name on my agenda and experienced a warm and comfortable feeling in my heart and mind. I began, "Ladies and gentlemen, today I think it's important to remember that while we're here to honor a football, baseball, and basketball coach, Riverview High School is an institution of learning that exists to prepare young people for the real world today and tomorrow. I doubt if there's anyone here who is an alumnus of Riverview who doesn't remember Mrs. Grimes' English Literature class." There were a few cheers and a few good-natured groans from the crowd. I continued, "Mrs. Grimes and Coach Edwards both believed in the power and validity of student athletes. Please welcome our own Mrs. Edna Grimes."

As the crowd applauded, Edna Grimes approached the podium with all the grace and dignity that an 80-year-old with a fear of public speaking could muster. She began, "Mr. Lucas, I want to thank you for that wonderful introduction, and I am proud to be here to share a few words and thoughts about my friend and colleague Mason G. Edwards. He was always very proud of the fact that the G stood for Geoffrey, and he shared that spelling with Geoffrey Chaucer who wrote *The Canterbury Tales*."

She looked at the generations of students she had introduced to the great thoughts and ideas expressed in the world of classic literature and continued, "For those of you who read *The Canterbury Tales* in my class, and for those of you who were *supposed* to read it and didn't..." The stadium erupted in good-natured laughter. She continued, "*The Canterbury Tales* was written over six hundred years ago by Geoffery Chaucer. He wrote of a diverse group of travelers making their way from London to Canterbury to visit a shrine. Coach Edwards loved the stories of the various travelers because he felt like it was a sports team involved in a great game. There were a variety of players with different talents and abilities all trying to reach the same goal." She paused for effect and seemed more comfortable in her role as a teacher giving a lecture.

She explained, "Coach Edwards and I both believed that we were teammates with different talents and abilities moving toward the same destination. My realm was my classroom, and my tools were the works of great writers. Coach Edwards felt that he was a teacher as well, but his classroom was not in the east wing of Riverview High School. It was in this stadium, the basketball field house, and the baseball diamond. We felt that our mission was to help each of you discover your own quest and equip you for the journey.

"As I have sat here on stage and listened to those who preceded me here at the podium, I can confidently proclaim that the coach discharged his duty, met every challenge, and succeeded with flying colors." Like a great teacher, she allowed pause for emphasis, then continued.

"Although Coach Edwards and I always saw academics and athletics as mutually beneficial, there were times when they could have conflicted. On more than one occasion, I had to call the coach and let him know that one of his players was failing in my class and would not be eligible to play on Friday night. The coach never asked for favors or to cut any corners. He simply wanted to know what extra effort his player could make to pull up his grade."

Edna Grimes smiled remembering a long-ago scene and shared her thoughts. "As a young person when I imagined myself teaching English literature, I never saw myself sitting in a locker room before a game with a six-foot-five, two-hundred-eighty-pound defensive tackle in full uniform who was reciting one of Shakespeare's sonnets from memory." The crowd burst into laughter at the scene she described.

Mrs. Grimes nodded and continued. "You'll be happy to know that the player in question recited the Bard's work admirably and played well that night getting two quarterback sacks and recovering a fumble." Applause could be heard throughout the stadium as if the football game were taking place in front of them instead of being shared as a memory from decades before.

Edna Grimes shared thoughts of her old friend and colleague. She told everyone assembled that the coach was not just a casual student, he was passionate about books. She remembered he had often said, "All leaders are readers." He often quoted his special friend who was actually named Charlie Tremendous Jones who wrote and stated, "You'll be the same person you are today five years from now except for the people you meet and the books you read."

Edna shared her long-ago memories, "The coach and I often exchanged books and discussed them during my planning hour or before his practices began. There are probably only a few of you here old enough to remember that when I was awaiting the birth of each of my three kids, Coach Mason G. Edwards stepped in and taught my classes. He did such a great job, I cut my maternity leave short in fear of losing my position." Everyone laughed good naturedly imagining the coach as the English literature teacher at Riverview High School.

The elderly instructor appeared thoughtful and continued, "Coach Edwards loved classic literature with epic heroes. He was fond of Ulysses and Don Quixote. He often listened to the soundtrack from the Broadway adaptation of Don Quixote and was constantly drawn to the song 'The Impossible Dream.'" Everyone could almost hear that classic showtune as they sat in the stadium remembering their coach and old friend.

Edna reached down to a shelf built into the podium and withdrew a large, well-worn leather notebook. She opened the book and turned the pages lovingly, lost in thought, then she spoke, "Mason G. Edwards was not just a student, a teacher, or a coach. He was an observer of people and a builder of successful lives. He believed that thoughts could change things, but the only way to deliver thoughts are the words we speak and hear. Many years ago, with his permission, I began capturing some of his thoughts and the words he used to deliver them in order to change the course of countless young people's lives." The crowd seemed to smile in understanding as each person thought of some of the coach's words that had changed their lives.

Edna ran her finger down a page and read several quotes.

"Only a few plays in a game really matter, but since we don't know which ones, we have to give a maximum effort all the time; all it takes to win is all you've got; and you change your life when you change your mind.

"These quotes and hundreds more have impacted all of us who encountered the coach personally here in Riverview...but no one other than his beloved wife Margaret and I have seen this manuscript." Edna Grimes allowed a pregnant pause to linger in the stadium, then announced, "But tonight, I believe it's both proper and fitting to announce that later this year, this treasured manuscript will be released as a book entitled, *Playbook for Success and Game Plan for Life*. The book will be described as the compiled thoughts and words of Coach Mason G. Edwards."

Thunderous applause echoed throughout the Riverview football stadium. Mrs. Edna Grimes smiled with satisfaction as she closed the manuscript on the podium before her. She concluded, "I will leave you with a favorite poem from my colleague and friend. It is entitled 'Cornerstones.'"

A few people in the crowd and some seated on stage nodded in recognition while everyone looked on with rapt attention as the beloved English teacher recited from memory:

> If I am to dream, let me dream magnificently.
>
> Let me dream grand and lofty
> thoughts and ideals
>
> That are worthy of me and my best efforts.
>
> If I am to strive, let me strive mightily.
>
> Let me spend myself and my very being
>
> In a quest for that magnificent dream.
>
> And, if I am to stumble, let me
> stumble but persevere.
>
> Let me learn, grow, and expand myself
> to join the battle renewed—
>
> Another day and another day and another day.

If I am to win, as I must, let me do so
with honor, humility, and gratitude

For those people and things that
have made winning possible

And so very sweet.

For each of us has been given life
as an empty plot of ground

With four cornerstones.

These four cornerstones are the ability to dream,

The ability to strive,

The ability to stumble but persevere,

And the ability to win.

The common man sees his plot
of ground as little more

Than a place to sit and ponder the
things that will never be.

But the uncommon man sees his
plot of ground as a castle,

A cathedral,

A place of learning and healing.

> For the uncommon man understands
> that in these four cornerstones
>
> The Almighty has given us
> anything—and everything.

The crowd emotionally applauded in response to their thoughts and memories of their beloved coach and friend.

7

Winning Through Overcoming

"Excellence becomes possible when we get over the notion that life is fair."
—Coach Mason G. Edwards

The ovation swelled to a crescendo as Edna Grimes walked away from the podium lovingly cradling the treasured manuscript in her arms. She smiled as she passed by me and whispered, "Mr. Lucas, I know the coach and Margaret would want you to have one of the first copies of the book." I thanked her sincerely as I was already anticipating what I knew would be a great book.

I knelt beside Billy Reynolds who was scheduled to be the next speaker and asked him, "Do you need anything special or is there anything I can do for you?"

He smiled confidently and responded, "No, sir. I think we've got it. Is there anything I can do for you?"

I chuckled and turned toward the podium. I was fully aware of the fact that Billy Reynolds regularly spoke to gatherings larger than this, but I always wanted to help him in any way I could. I stood at the podium, glanced at the brief introduction, and began.

"Billy Reynolds is known far and wide as someone who has motivated and inspired a generation. He is a bestselling author with several of his novels being turned into movies. He regularly speaks to millions of people at arena events, writes a syndicated column widely read in newspapers and magazines around the world, and is heard on two national radio programs each week."

I looked up from my notes and spoke from my heart. "Billy, nevertheless, is one of us. He keeps Riverview in his heart as he takes the thoughts, ideas, and concepts he learned here and shares them around the world. Please welcome the one and only Billy Reynolds."

There was a thunderous round of applause as Billy Reynolds stood and strode to the podium with the aid of a guide dog, a beautiful silver-white German Shepherd.

Billy Reynolds placed his hands lightly on the podium, nodded to the crowd, smiled, and began. "I am indeed Billy Reynolds from Riverview, and while I'm not sure I can live up to Athletic Director Lucas's glowing introduction, his words will give me something to aspire to." Billy Reynolds nodded to me as if he could see exactly where I was sitting, then gestured to the guide dog seated beside him.

"This is my friend, traveling companion, and advisor, Cooper." The beautiful dog got a round of applause and Billy turned to where Mrs. Edna Grimes was sitting and continued, "Mrs. Grimes, you'll be pleased to know that, although I didn't read *The Last of the Mohicans* when I was supposed to in your class, I listened to the audio version years later and fell in love with it. To the extent that this wonderful creature..." He gestured again to the dog then continued, "...is named Cooper in tribute to Mr. James Fenimore Cooper.

"As a bestselling author, I'm embarrassed to admit to those of you in my hometown, that when I could read with my eyes like you do, I don't know that I ever read an entire book cover to cover. After losing my sight and learning how to live as a blind person, I discovered audiobooks and high-speed listening. I can honestly say that I don't know anyone who has read as many books as I have, and becoming a reader made me want to become a writer and gave me a love and appreciation for what Mrs. Grimes was trying to teach us all in her English literature class."

Billy Reynolds paused thoughtfully and explained, "It's wonderful to be back here in Riverview because it's one of the few places I remember seeing with my own eyes. I was a first baseman on Coach Edwards' baseball team. I had thoughts of playing pro ball because my dad made it to the Minor Leagues back in his day." Billy Reynolds gestured to his left and announced, "Many of you have been kind enough to refer to me as Mr. Reynolds since I arrived back in town a couple of days ago. But right now, I would like to introduce you to the real Mr. Reynolds, my father, Fred Reynolds."

The crowd applauded politely, and Billy continued, "If everyone in the world had been raised by Fred Reynolds, taught by Edna Grimes, and coached by Mason G. Edwards, I would have to find something different to talk about, write about, and make movies about."

Billy Reynolds paused, sighed deeply, and seemed to travel back in time. He told of how much he loved playing baseball for the coach, but everyone on the team seemed to notice that late in each game, his performance declined. The initial thought was that he was lazy or just got tired, but Coach Edwards was the one who discovered that the afternoon games often carried on to the evening when it began to get dark, and he realized his first baseman struggled to see well enough to catch or hit the ball.

The coach met with Billy's parents and arranged for an appointment with a renowned ophthalmologist at the state capital. The expert physician sadly informed Billy Reynolds, his parents, and Coach Edwards that Billy's sight would continue to decline, and he would be totally blind within the next few years. Billy spoke as if he had just gotten that fateful prognosis, "I didn't know what to say or do. Coach Edwards hugged me and told me he would see me at practice.

"The next day, Coach Edwards and I gave the bad news to the team, and the coach told me to wait on the bench until after practice. After everyone had left, Coach told me to follow him, and we walked into this football stadium through that south gate." Billy pointed directly to the spot he was describing and recalled the coach's words. "Son, you've been dealt a tough hand. But I am a firm believer that opportunities come disguised as problems, and since you've got a big problem, you need to start looking for a big opportunity."

Billy paused and explained that the coach had recited one of his favorite quotes from the renowned author Napoleon Hill, "Every adversity, every failure, every heartbreak, carries with it the seed of an equal or greater benefit."

Billy told how he had stood next to the coach while the football team was practicing. At one point, they stood in front of where the offense was running their plays. Billy remembered, "Coach asked me if I could see well enough to follow the ball as the quarterback handed it off to the running back. I told him I was able to follow it, and he just smiled and nodded. At the end of practice, he told me to stay with him as the football team gathered around."

Billy spoke as if he were Coach Edwards on that long-ago day. "Gentlemen, good practice today. I think we'll be ready to give a good account of ourselves Friday night when we are over at Central High. Meanwhile, I think you all know Billy Reynolds. He's our new defensive end." The crowd applauded Coach Edwards' heroic gesture.

Billy continued, "I may not have been the best defensive end the Riverview Pioneers ever had, but I wasn't the worst. In fact, I made all-conference my senior year, and the coach told a newspaper reporter that I may have been the only player in history to hit a home run while playing defensive end." The crowd laughed and cheered.

Billy continued, "As many of you know, Coach Edwards believed his duties as coach extended far beyond practices and game days. He was by my side as the world faded out and I went blind. He never pitied me and never expected anything less than excellence from me. I remember when I was going to a clinic two days a week to work with a mobility instructor who taught me how to navigate the world with a white cane or with my friend Cooper."

He paused and gestured to the beautiful guide dog by his side and told of how he had arrived one day for his mobility appointment but the door to the instructor's office was closed. Just before he knocked, he heard the unmistakable and highly motivated voice of Coach Edwards coming from inside the office, "Yes, ma'am, I'm sure you're a good instructor and you've dealt with hundreds of blind people, but you haven't dealt with anyone like Billy Reynolds. This kid is special, and if you will push him hard, he'll give you the best performance you ever saw."

The emotion of that long-ago moment swept over the crowd. Billy described his hard work with the mobility instructor and the fact that the coach never knew that he had overheard the conversation in the office. Billy remembered that when his mobility training was over, he got a Braille letter from the instructor that read, "Dear Billy, I was told by someone that you had the potential to be one of my best students, and I have to admit he was right."

Billy concluded his remarks in his familiar role as motivator, "Ladies and gentlemen, there is only one true fitting memorial for Coach Mason G. Edwards, and that is for each of us to dream our biggest dreams, give our maximum effort, and live our best lives. If we can do that, our beloved coach and friend will have accomplished his life's mission."

8

Winning Through Urgency

"In the world of success, there's no such thing as someday. Today's the day."
—Coach Mason G. Edwards

The thunderous standing ovation for Billy Reynolds' tribute to Coach Edwards was more reminiscent of a motivational rally than a memorial service. Billy stepped back from the podium and waved to the crowd. On cue, Cooper waved his paw to them. It was obvious that the two of them had done this many times before.

As I glanced at my notes, preparing to introduce the next speaker, I blurted, "Wow. I'm glad I don't have to follow Billy and Cooper here today." The crowd chuckled and I began, "As much fun as we are having and as many fond memories as we are enjoying, it's impossible on this special night to forget our great loss and what a void the passing of Coach Mason G. Edwards leaves in all our hearts and lives.

"Now I want to introduce someone who had a unique relationship with the coach and can give us a powerful perspective. Dr. Bernard Olson is a renowned oncologist who has done cutting-edge research and has written extensively on new and improved treatments for cancer. Please welcome him."

If you were casting a movie featuring an eminent physician who combined cutting-edge science with compassionate care, the actor would look and act like Dr. Olson. He was a tall, lean man with a full head of white hair. The glasses he wore made him seem like an intellectual, but at the same time, made him more human and approachable. The doctor confidently strode across the stage and took his place at the podium.

He began, "I've been in practice for thirty-two years, and for the last decade have worked in the research hospital at the state capital. The patients I see have been referred by other doctors when the traditional cancer treatments are no longer working." He paused and looked intently at the massive audience gathered in the stadium. He shrugged and continued, "You may be wondering if I speak at memorial services for all my patients. I have to admit this is the first memorial service or celebration of life I have ever attended for a patient in my entire career. It is an unusual situation, but your Coach Edwards was an unusual man."

Many in the crowd smiled knowingly while others nodded in agreement. Dr. Olson went on to explain that from the moment Coach Mason G. Edwards arrived in his office, he and his entire staff knew that they were encountering something totally new, unusual, and quite special.

The doctor gave his best Coach Edwards' impression of their first meeting, "Doctor, it's a pleasure to meet you, and I am told you are a top performer in your field with a solid track record, but I want to make sure we're on the same page. I will leave treating the disease and attacking the cancer to you and your teammates, but I would like us to focus on attacking every day of my life with power, passion, and persistence."

The doctor collected his thoughts, and said, "It would be difficult to describe the impact that Coach Edwards had on my staff, my patients, and me. Thankfully, you all knew him far better than I did, so you understand the phenomenon. Everyone the coach encountered was somehow altered or changed. My office manager, who greets patients and oversees them while they're in the waiting room, told me of a conversation Coach Edwards had with a young woman facing a serious diagnosis and a somewhat bleak future. The coach introduced himself and asked her about her condition, her treatment, and her life. The young woman emotionally told about the painful treatment and her hopeless situation. Coach Edwards changed her attitude and her life by letting her know that it's not as important how many days we have left in our life, but what matters is how much life we have left in our days. He described getting a sense of urgency and treating every day as if it were a gift because that is what it is. The coach somehow turned my waiting room into a locker room before a championship game.

"He told my cancer patient about when his basketball team was playing for the state championship one year, and the opposing team had a seven-foot-tall center. The coach described his players complaining that it wasn't fair. Ironically, the coach actually agreed with his team and took them into the film room replaying previous games featuring the seven-foot center. The coach pointed out details of how the very tall young man was playing and told his players they were right. It really wasn't fair because as they could see, the seven-foot-tall player couldn't dribble or shoot with his left hand. Coach Edwards' team won that championship by forcing their seven-foot opponent to catch the basketball, dribble, and shoot with his left hand. The coach summarized by explaining that we always find what we're looking for. If we're looking for pain, suffering, and defeat, we will find it. In much the same way, if we're looking for success, victory, and joy, we will discover that it is equally available." The crowd respectfully applauded the coach's words.

The doctor continued. "I'm told that Coach Edwards stayed in touch with that young lady and made a lasting difference for her and her family. During the almost two years we treated your coach, his main focus was on his teams and all of you. He made sure that my staff and I all had the schedule of his upcoming practices and games so we could schedule his treatment days in such a way that he could perform at the highest possible level in his role as a coach. He lived every day doing exactly what he wanted to do. Although the cancer eventually took his life, I can assure you, it never took his pride, his dignity, or his quest for excellence."

Emotion seemed to flood over the doctor as he described the life and death of someone who was much more a friend than a patient. The doctor announced, "Now I'm going to share something that is highly unique and unusual. There is a support group made up of my cancer patients. They have met each week for years to help one another through the emotional difficulties of the disease and the treatment. It won't surprise you to know that from the first time Coach Edwards attended the support group to this very day, it has never been quite the same."

The doctor looked at the large screens behind him and stated, "Right now, some of the patients who came to know and love Coach Mason G. Edwards wanted to share a few of their thoughts."

The image of a middle-aged woman wearing a Riverview Pioneers ballcap appeared on the screen. She spoke, "My name is Betty. In our group, we only use first names, and in the case of your beloved Coach Mason G. Edwards, he was simply known to all of us as Coach. I will admit that I know very little about football, baseball, or basketball, but Coach taught me how to be a winner and expect the best out of every situation and how I could maximize every day of my life. My family and I are grateful, and I just wanted to share in this special tribute."

Her image faded and a young boy of seven or eight appeared on the screen. He excitedly spoke, "My name is Eric. I used to tell everyone that I was a blood cancer patient, but Coach helped me to understand I don't define myself by a disease. Cancer is something I have, but it's not who I am. Coach was really cool." Many in the audience smiled through their tears as they witnessed the brave and emotional young boy. He continued, "Coach brought us hats and jerseys and footballs and all kinds of cool stuff. I used to never think about the future, but now I think I'd like to grow up and be a coach."

Eric's image faded from the screen and was replaced by an elderly African American man. "My name is George. I spent twenty years in the military, served in three wars, and traveled around the world. But I can tell you, I never saw anyone quite like Coach. A lot of people talk a good game, but he lived it. No one from the outside could have ever impacted our group, but Coach was one of us. He always encouraged us, challenged us, and made us better."

Dr. Olson resumed his place at the podium and announced, "There is one more of my patients who wanted to speak at this very special event. Please welcome Terri."

The crowd applauded politely as a college-aged woman approached the podium. She hugged Dr. Olson, looked at the vast audience, and began. "Coach always told us we should challenge ourselves every day to do something that makes us scared or uncomfortable. He said, if you face the fear, it goes away."

She smiled brightly and continued, "Once again, he was right because I'm standing here and thousands of you are sitting out there. I've never done anything like this before, and I was terrified to come here, but I was more terrified to let the fear control me. Coach always said, the things you can do, you should do; but things you can't do, you simply must do. Otherwise, you'll never be any bigger than you are right now and tomorrow cannot be better than today.

"Coach Edwards was a great reader, and he gave books to all of us. I will always treasure the copy of *Man's Search for Meaning* by Dr. Viktor Frankl that he gave to me. It's a book about a man who lost his family and business during World War II. He was put into a concentration camp with little hope to survive. He came to realize that his captors might be able to take away his freedom and his future, but they could never touch his joy and dignity."

Terri reached into her pocket and took out a worn book. She opened it and read what had been written on the inside front cover, "Terri, you are a winner and a bright, shining light for everyone in your world. You make a difference to everyone around you—especially me. Today's the day, Coach Mason G. Edwards." Terri closed the book, nodded to the crowd, and left the stage.

9

Winning Through Belief

*"Our achievements are only
limited by our beliefs."*
—Coach Mason G. Edwards

As Dr. Bernard Olson made his final remarks, Terri approached the stairs leading down from the stage but stopped when she saw me. She said, "Mr. Lucas, I wanted to meet you. Coach told me all about you." I smiled and nodded. She continued, "He said everyone needs to find someone in their life who will go into battle with them and celebrate the great times of life. He told me that you had always been there for him, taking care of all the details and encouraging him to be better than he was. Coach told me I needed to find someone like you."

Tears filled her eyes as she continued, "I found my own Gill Lucas in the form of my best friend, Susan. We have celebrated the ups and downs together, and she has made me better."

I was flooded with emotion and unable to speak, so I just nodded. Terri smiled at me and asked, "Can I hug you?" I nodded again and we embraced. She turned and walked away, and I knew that I would never be the same. Even after his passing, my lifelong friend and colleague, Mason Edwards, was encouraging me, challenging me, and making me better.

The applause throughout the stadium alerted me that Dr. Olson had concluded his tribute, and I prepared myself for the next introduction. Throughout my professional life with Coach Edwards, I learned that everyone is special, but there are a handful of people who are extra special.

I glanced at my agenda as if I hadn't already been thinking about the next introduction all day. I had been told that Thesa

Loving was waiting, with her assistants and security people, in a private room under the stadium until it was time for her tribute to Coach Edwards. She wasn't being some kind of diva or recluse; she just wanted the evening to be focused on Coach Mason G. Edwards instead of her. We had thought that her return to Riverview had remained a secret, but when banners proclaiming, "Welcome home, Thesa Loving" started appearing around town that afternoon, we knew the word was out. Thankfully, the media hounds and paparazzi had behaved, for the most part, befitting the solemn occasion.

With the exception of observing her image projected 40 feet tall on movie screens, I had not seen Thesa Loving since she graduated from Riverview High School 15 years earlier. My introduction simply stated what everyone in the stadium already knew, "Thesa Loving is known around the world as the award-winning star of stage and screen. She has been called a cultural icon, but here in Riverview, we simply call her one of our own."

Thesa Loving glided onto the stage accompanied by thunderous applause. Everyone on the platform that evening had been in the glow of both the stadium lights and the special spotlights in use for the tribute, but Thesa seemed to glow from within. I stood at the podium applauding with the rest of the crowd watching her approach. She gave me that million-dollar smile of hers and hugged me warmly saying, "It's good to see you, Mr. Lucas. Thanks for the great introduction."

I stammered, "You're welcome, and can you call me Gill?"

She laughed knowingly and responded, "I really doubt it."

As the crowd settled into their seats, Thesa Loving spoke to them. "It's good to be home, and I am proud to be a Riverview Pioneer." The crowd roared its approval.

She continued, "It's been said countless times in the media that I came from an obscure no-name place and took the world by storm, but you and I know differently. Riverview is one of the best-kept secrets and most valuable treasures in the world, and certainly in my life. Movie critics have accused me of adopting a Hollywood stage name, but those of you who grew up with me here in Riverview know that my parents Herb and Sally gave me the name Thesa."

She looked to her right and pointed to a middle-aged couple sitting on the first row and said, "Mom and Dad, stand up." She smiled at them as the crowd welcomed her parents with a warm round of applause.

Thesa continued, "As I said, they gave me the name Thesa, and as for my last name Loving, it came to me as the result of a failed early marriage. You golfers will understand when I call it a Mulligan marriage. That's simply a golf shot that doesn't go the way you want it to, so you get out another golf ball and start over. I didn't get anything from that relationship other than my last name, for which I'm grateful."

The crowd nodded and chuckled warmly. Thesa had the same ability on that stage that she had on the movie screen to get people to feel comfortable with her and like her immediately. She gazed around the stadium at the entire crowd, smiled, shrugged, and admitted, "It won't surprise you to learn that I never played football, basketball, or baseball for Coach Edwards." We all laughed at the irony as we pictured this international superstar and movie icon wearing football gear.

She told of how one of the first things in her life she was really good at was being a cheerleader. She became the head cheerleader her junior year and was eagerly anticipating becoming a senior and filling that role one more time. But the director of the cheerleading program, due to pressure from cheer competitions, made a rule that all the senior girls would have to be able to do a standing backflip if they wanted to be part of the squad. Thesa had a forlorn look as she remembered, "I simply couldn't do it. I tried everything and only succeeded at getting bumps and bruises over my entire body.

"Because I was the head cheerleader, I had a key to the gym so that summer, I secretly came into the school and began practicing on my own. Unbeknownst to me, Coach Edwards also came into the school gym throughout the summer to watch game films, work on his playbook, and get ready for the football season. Well, Coach apparently heard what he thought was an intruder down the hall, so he came to check it out carrying a baseball bat with him."

The crowd smiled with anticipation, and Thesa told of how the coach rushed around the corner brandishing the baseball bat and yelled, "Who are you and what are you doing?" Thesa smiled at the memory and said, "I had no idea who was yelling and threatening me with a baseball bat until I recognized the coach at the same moment he recognized me. We both took a deep breath and just stood there staring at one another." We could all picture that uncomfortable confrontation.

Thesa remembered the Coach's words, "I know who you are, but I still don't know what you're doing here."

The crowd seemed to lean forward in anticipation at the long-ago memory being shared by a master storyteller. Thesa recalled, "I was embarrassed, but I told him about my backflip dilemma, and he seemed to ponder the problem for a few moments."

Thesa once again remembered the coach's words, "Well, we simply need to address the situation. We know the goal, we have a timeframe, and now we're going to devise a plan and implement it to ensure our success."

Thesa became emotional as she spoke, "I will never forget how the coach immediately identified my problem as *our* problem, and the plan was *our* plan, not just my own. He put together a stretching and weightlifting regimen that nearly killed me. We worked all summer just the two of us alone in the gym."

Thesa pointed at a spot beyond the far end of the stadium where the Riverview gymnasium still stood. She told of the fateful day, a week before school started, when the coach burst in for one of their private summer sessions and confidently declared, "Today's the day we are going to do a backflip."

Thesa let the tension build throughout the stadium like a world class actress, and then triumphantly declared, "And ladies and gentlemen, that day I did indeed perform a standing backflip." The crowd applauded as if she had just hit a homerun.

"Coach never told anyone about all our sessions that summer. I was proud to be the head cheerleader for my senior year. That fall, Coach Edwards' football team made it to the state championship game. It was close throughout the first three quarters, but then our Riverview Pioneers pulled ahead in the fourth quarter." The crowd cheered as if the game were happening at that very moment.

Thesa continued, "Coach Mason G. Edwards was one of the most powerful forces in my life. He not only gave me the ability and the confidence to perform, but he gave me the first stage that I performed on. With less than two minutes left in the state championship game, we were ahead by a touchdown and had the ball. All the Pioneers needed to do was take a knee and run out the clock. With 37 seconds to go, the fans, the band, and we cheerleaders were getting ready to storm the field in victory, and then Coach Edwards inexplicably called a time-out. We in the movie business believe that a picture is worth a thousand words, and a movie has a thousand pictures."

Thesa stepped away from the podium as the lights in the stadium dimmed, and the scene from the long-ago state championship football game was projected onto the giant screens. The coach did, indeed, call a time-out and signal his players to the sideline. He then stepped forward and motioned to Thesa and the cheerleaders to move to the center of the field in the packed state championship stadium. They performed a flawless routine that ended with Thesa Loving executing a perfect standing backflip. The coach stood and applauded as all his players joined the standing ovation.

As the image on the screen faded, that same ovation could be heard as Thesa stepped back to the podium. A tear ran down her cheek as she spoke, "I will always remember at the end of the graduation ceremony that year, Coach Edwards sought me out, congratulated me, and gave me a big hug." She stood there as the memories seemed to flood around her, then she recited the coach's words that established the course of her life, "Thesa, don't ever forget, a person who can do a backflip can do anything."

The crowd was struck with emotion. Some smiled, some cried, and others bowed their heads reflecting on that special moment. Thesa concluded, "Over the years, I have been in many daunting situations negotiating with Broadway producers and movie studios, but I always remind myself that I can do a backflip."

10

Winning Through Integrity

"All success begins and ends with keeping your word."
—Coach Mason G. Edwards

Thesa Loving smiled and waved at the crowd as if she were walking the red carpet at the Academy Awards ceremony. She stepped over to me, smiled, and said, "Gill, thanks for letting me come here and share."

I laughed and responded, "I thought you couldn't call me Gill."

She hugged me and whispered, "I can do a backflip, so I can do anything."

The crowd was energized as she left the stage, and I couldn't help but worry about anyone having to follow her, but I thought that the duo listed on my agenda would be up to the task.

Martin Finn and Steve Atwell were rarely seen or even spoken of separately. They were lifelong friends and business partners. Everyone for miles around Riverview was familiar with the Finn-Atwell Bank, Insurance Agency, Construction Company, and many other successful enterprises.

I stood at the podium and declared, "If they ever change the name of Riverview, I think we should probably call our town Finn-Atwell since everything is already named after them."

The crowd laughed good-naturedly as I welcomed the two of them to the podium. Steve Atwell was immaculately dressed in a suit with a muted tie appropriate for a memorial service, but his partner Marty Finn was wearing a Riverview High School letterman's jacket. I shook hands with each of them, and Martin Finn began to speak.

"We want to thank everyone for the opportunity to be here tonight and talk about the man who taught us most of what we know and made us who we are."

Steve Atwell pointed at his partner and quipped, "You ever notice how this guy goes right for the microphone every time."

When the crowd's laughter died down, Steve Atwell continued, "One of the great joys in life is making fun of my best friend and partner."

Martin Finn nodded and admitted, "We weren't always partners or even friends." He glanced at Steve Atwell who nodded for him to continue. "It was our sophomore year, and we were both trying to get the last spot on Coach Edwards' varsity basketball team." He stepped back and let his partner Steve Atwell continue.

"Marty and I were fierce competitors and rivals before we were anything else. The day that changed our lives happened when, after practice, I was going to get a Coke from the machine and Marty told me if I would get him one, he would return the favor the next day."

Marty stepped forward and spoke as if they had choreographed their presentation. "Steve gave me a Coke, but the next day in practice he beat up on me in a rebounding drill, so after practice, I decided to spend my extra money getting a candy bar to have with my Coke instead of buying the one I had promised to him. When he confronted me about it, I just laughed at him, and the next thing I knew he was beating me up again right there in the locker room just like he had done during the rebounding drill at practice."

Steve continued, "Well, we were beating each other up pretty good when Coach Edwards came in and separated us. We were such obscure players that he had to ask our names. I told him that I had bought Marty a Coke the day before and he promised to pay me back, but he didn't."

Marty took over, "Coach gave me a look that causes my blood to run cold to this very day." The crowd shifted uncomfortably as many of them were familiar with that look.

The coach had asked Martin Finn if the story was true and when he nodded yes, the coach spoke memorable words of wisdom, "You boys may or may not ever learn how to play basketball, but you are, for sure, going to learn how to have integrity. If your word's not good, nothing else matters. Throughout your life and to the very end of it, the best thing you can be known for is that your word was good, and you lived with integrity."

Steve Atwell spoke. "Then the coach turned to me and asked how much a Coke cost. I told him fifty cents. He reached into his pocket and handed Marty two quarters."

Marty remembered, "Coach told me to never sell my integrity for a million dollars and certainly not for fifty cents. Then he told me to buy a Coke for Steve and make it right."

Steve continued, "Marty brought me a Coke, apologized, and shook my hand." The crowd applauded as the two middle-aged men shook hands again standing at the podium, then warmly hugged one another. Steve declared, "We've been best friends and partners ever since. In our lives and in our businesses, we're not perfect, and sometimes we make mistakes. But we always make it right and move forward in integrity."

Marty paused poignantly, then shared his memories. "We worked really hard to make the team and somehow the coach adjusted the lineup so we both got to play varsity basketball. We each played enough minutes to win our letterman's jacket." The crowd cheered and applauded. Marty gestured to his jacket and continued, "You may have noticed I wore my letterman's jacket tonight."

His partner Steve cut in and quipped, "It's bad enough to dress inappropriately. You don't have to point it out to everyone."

The crowd roared with laughter and Marty continued, "Well, folks, once again, the true significance of the situation and the higher standard went right over the head of my partner." Everyone laughed and the two guys smiled good-naturedly at one another.

Martin sighed and struggled with his emotions as he shared, "Earning this letterman's jacket has always been a big deal to me. For that reason, every year when they present the basketball players with their letters, I attend the ceremony wearing my own jacket. Many of you will remember a special young man and basketball player here in Riverview named Marcus Robbins. Marcus was permanently injured in a horrible accident and lost the use of both of his hands.

"Apparently, when the coach visited him in the hospital, Marcus expressed that one of his biggest disappointments was that he wouldn't be part of the team and get his letterman's jacket. Unbeknownst to everyone, Coach Edwards told him there was a position for a team manager who would keep the score sheet, organize the game films, and take care of all the details. Marcus fulfilled that role throughout his senior year and came to the awards ceremony expecting to get his letter that would be later sewn onto his jacket.

"Well, apparently whoever ordered the letters that year wasn't aware of the arrangement the coach had made, and the coach realized he didn't have a letter for Marcus Robbins." The emotion of that moment pressed down on the crowd as Marty continued.

"Then, the coach looked over at me standing there wearing my letterman's jacket and motioned for me to step out into the hall. Without any explanation or even a greeting, Coach Edwards took out his pocketknife and cut my letter off my jacket." The crowd laughed as they visualized the absurd moment. Martin Finn continued, "In fairness, as coach was running back into the room where the ceremony was held, he told me he would replace my letter—which he indeed did."

The crowd applauded and Marty stepped out from behind the podium and explained, "I took that letter the coach gave me and put it on a new letterman's jacket that I wear. And except for this occasion tonight, this jacket is on display in my office at the bank in the trophy case." He pointed to a small patch where the letter had been cut away and the threads in the shape of the 'R' for Riverview could still be seen. A camera zoomed in on the spot and projected the image onto the giant screens. The patch read, "Keeping your word is sometimes inconvenient, difficult, and challenging, but it's always worth it."

As applause thundered from the crowd, Martin Finn smiled proudly and concluded the story. "It's amazing what happened in our lives due to a fifty-cent Coke long ago and a special coach who cared about young men and integrity."

Marty Finn sheepishly admitted, "I didn't realize until this very moment that I still owe Coach Edwards fifty cents." Thunderous laughter could be heard throughout the stadium, and he continued, "Well, to try to make up for my delinquent payment for a long-owed debt, tonight I would like to announce that, outside of the entrance to the locker room, a bronze statue of Coach Edwards will stand in order to remind us all to live with integrity." An image of the statue flashed onto the screens above the platform. The crowd applauded their approval.

Steve Atwell continued the announcement. "Furthermore, the Finn-Atwell Bank will be endowing a Memorial Integrity Award and Scholarship that will be given each year to the player that exhibits the principles of honesty and integrity established by Coach Mason G. Edwards."

Martin Finn concluded, "As the coach told me those many years ago, there's nothing better than to live your entire life being known as a person of honor and integrity. The coach certainly succeeded on that front, and if we can all apply his lessons in our personal and professional lives, Coach Mason G. Edwards will not have passed this way in vain."

The two friends and partners shook my hand and thanked me as they left the stage. I was struck by the fact that, during my more than half a century friendship and working relationship with Coach Edwards, I had occasionally questioned his judgment and once in a while wondered about a few of his decisions. But not once had I ever doubted his integrity.

11

Winning Through Effort

"When you think you've done your best and have no more to give, you will find there is still more in your tank."
—Coach Mason G. Edwards

It had been quite an evening to that point. We had reveled in old memories and special times as well as consoled one another in the loss and sorrow we felt in that moment. So I was looking forward to planting a seed that would bear fruit in the future. I stood at the podium, took a letter out of my jacket pocket and unfolded it in front me. I explained, "Ladies and gentlemen, I received this letter from Coach Edwards' attorney shortly after his passing. I got permission from Mrs. Edwards to read it to you at this time, and it will serve as my introduction of our next speaker."

I looked down at the now familiar letter and felt the same wave of emotions I had experienced the first time I had read it. I recited those powerful and poignant words, "To my beloved friend and treasured colleague Gill Lucas. If you're reading this letter, it means I have graduated to the next level, and I'm playing in the big leagues." The crowd smiled and a few chuckles could be heard as I continued, "As you know, Jeff Stewart was one of my favorite baseball players when he was on the Riverview Pioneers team years ago. He was never the biggest, fastest, or most talented player, but he was a great teammate and made practicing and playing baseball fun for everyone. I've always believed that high school sports should be fun so that players will pay attention and stay dedicated allowing them to learn all the lessons that baseball, basketball, and football have to offer. After Jeff made us all proud here and distinguished himself as a professional ballplayer, he settled back in Riverview and has been my assistant baseball coach ever since.

"As I write these words, we are in the middle of a hotly contested baseball season. We have a good team that I feel is headed for the playoffs, but I don't believe I'm going to make it that long. So, I've already spoken to the school board, and as soon as you get this letter, please let Jeff and everyone know that our team is in good hands as they pursue the playoffs because Jeff Stewart is the new head baseball coach of the Riverview Pioneers."

I paused for the vigorous applause and concluded reading Coach Edwards' letter. "Gill, I want to thank you for handling this little assignment just like you handled thousands of them for me over the years. No one ever had a better friend or companion. The best is yet to come. And it's signed, Respectfully, Coach Mason G. Edwards."

I folded the letter and put it back into my pocket as the crowd cheered. Then, I announced, "Riverview Pioneer fans, please welcome our new head baseball coach, Jeff Stewart."

Jeff looked shocked and bewildered as he walked across the stage accompanied by thunderous applause. I hugged him and he muttered, "Thanks, Gill."

I assured him, "You deserve it, Coach."

The brand-new head baseball coach, Jeff Stewart, stood at the podium and gazed across the huge crowd. He began, "Well, Coach Edwards and Gill Lucas have always challenged, surprised, and amazed me, and they did it again tonight. Obviously, I came here with the intention of offering a tribute to my former coach and my boss, Mason G. Edwards. But now, as I think of him, I also consider our baseball team and the playoffs that are approaching." Jeff Stewart smiled and chuckled, then continued, "I imagine Coach had it planned that way."

Coach Jeff Stewart stood thoughtfully and reflected on his long-ago memories. "The first day I showed up for practice, Coach Edwards sat us all down in the dugout and told us that our best efforts would always be good enough, and it wasn't a player's job to win games; it was his job to maximize his talent. I thought he was trying to calm us down and take the pressure off, but little did I know how hard it was going to be to do my best and maximize my talent.

"As I stand here on this amazing occasion, my thoughts take me back to one hot, dusty practice during which I got a hit, flied out twice, and ended the scrimmage by grounding into a double play. After the practice, Coach sought me out in the locker room and said he would like to talk to me, so I should get dressed and meet him at home plate. I got dressed as fast as was humanly possible and rushed back out to the baseball diamond where the coach was indeed standing on home plate. He indicated that I should walk with him while we were talking, and he headed down the first base line."

Then, the new Coach Jeff Stewart spoke as he recited the words of his former coach Mason G. Edwards, "Jeff, I want to talk to you about practice today. There are only a few plays in any game that really matter. Unfortunately, I don't know when those plays are going to be, and neither do you. All we can do is give our maximum effort in every moment of every play."

Jeff Stewart then described how the coach had asked him how he thought he played during practice that day. Jeff recalled his response, "I shrugged and told the coach I felt good about getting a hit, but I hated that I grounded into a double play that ended our scrimmage. The coach just nodded, stepped on first base, turned, and began walking back down the baseline toward home plate."

Jeff Stewart described asking the coach if he was mad that he had grounded into a double play. He described how the coach had shaken his head no and explained, "Son, the best athletes and the most famous people who ever played the game of baseball all grounded into double plays many times. But the thing the great players always do that you didn't do today is give a maximum effort running to first base. I know it was hot and you were tired at the end of the scrimmage, but I stood there and watched you half-heartedly jog toward first base."

Coach Stewart lowered his head as if the incident had just happened, then recalled Coach Edwards' words. "You need to realize that if you follow pro baseball, you will see that about one in twenty ground balls are mishandled or dropped. If the batter runs with maximum effort to first base on those one in twenty plays, he will be safe. If he always plays with maximum effort, the statistics tell us he will be on base eight more times during a season than a player who half-heartedly jogs to first base after they hit a ground ball. Out of those eight extra times the great ball player is on base, he will score an average of three more times per season. This can easily make the difference in those three ballgames, and the average team that makes the playoffs qualifies by a margin of less than three games. Do you understand me, Jeff?"

Jeff Stewart paused reflectively, looked up at the crowd and continued, "I told the coach then that I did, indeed, understand just like I understood it for the rest of my career and to this very day.

"In my senior year here at Riverview High, I played in a game where I hit a ground ball that would have resulted in a double play, but I ran for all I was worth, and the shortstop didn't pick up the ball cleanly, so his throw was a half-second late which was the margin I needed to get on first base." The crowd applauded.

Jeff raised his hands and continued, "But that's not all. A few weeks later, I got a letter from a college scout from our state university who had been at that game. His letter informed me that they were offering me a college scholarship to play baseball, and he complimented me as he wrote in his letter what had really impressed him was the way I had run out the ground ball."

The crowd cheered the long-ago success of one of their favorite Pioneer players. He continued, "Folks, as Coach Edwards wrote in his letter to Gill, I wasn't the biggest, strongest, fastest, or best baseball player. But what gave me the chance to go to college, get my degree, then make my living playing pro ball, as well as coaching here at Riverview High, is the fact that one very special coach told me the key to life itself and every success, which is to always do your best and give a maximum effort."

He sighed and seemed to assume his new position announcing, "And now as the new head baseball coach here at Riverview High, I've got some really big shoes to fill. Thankfully, I've got the wisdom and inspiration he gave us all to draw upon.

"Coach always told me to set your goals with emotion, so you can rise above your current circumstances and abilities to strive for something better, and to establish your plan with logic so you can carry it out step by step beginning right where you are. And that is exactly what we'll be doing at baseball practice starting tomorrow."

12

Winning Through Relationships

"The most important things in our lives are the relationships we have with others."
—Coach Mason G. Edwards

I rushed onto the stage and shook hands with Coach Stewart. I wanted to connect with him before he left the podium as I had a presentation to make. I signaled for him to stay put as I announced to the crowd, "Before our head baseball coach Jeff Stewart gets away, I have a brief presentation to make." I handed him a package. So much had been happening to him in the last few minutes, he just stood there dumbstruck until I suggested, "Coach Stewart, you might want to open your package."

The crowd laughed, applauded, and waited in eager anticipation. Jeff Stewart opened the packet to reveal a brand-new coach's baseball jacket. Embroidered on the front, it said, "Jeff Stewart. Head Baseball Coach. Riverview Pioneers." I motioned for the coach to put on his jacket. He handed me his suit coat and donned his new coach's jacket that fit him perfectly. He turned so the audience could get a good look at it. They cheered enthusiastically.

I stood at the podium and announced, "Coach, before we let you go, I have one more brief presentation. It's a letter addressed to you." The crowd hushed and the new head baseball coach appeared curious and a bit bewildered.

I read, "Dear Coach Stewart. Congratulations on your new head coaching role. We are all very proud of you, and we are looking forward to the rest of the season. We would like to dedicate the rest of this year to Coach Mason G. Edwards. And it is signed by your entire baseball team."

The crowd stood and cheered, and I handed the coach the letter. He held it as if it were a priceless heirloom, glanced at it reverently, then waved to the crowd as he left the stage.

I stood at the podium and allowed the new head coach to soak up all the applause from his fans. I knew it was time for me to shift gears, and I wasn't quite sure how to make the transition.

That morning had begun for me with the graveside service for Coach Edwards. It was a private ceremony with only a handful of family members and close friends. I was proud to have been included. After the minister had shared some powerful and hopeful thoughts, I looked on as my beloved colleague and lifelong friend was lowered into his final resting place on a knoll overlooking the river. His headstone read, "Coach Mason G. Edwards. Beloved husband, treasured friend, and coach for life."

It seemed like very few words for such a giant human being, but maybe the giants among us need the fewest words as their deeds speak for themselves. I hugged Coach Edwards' widow before I left the graveside and asked her if she would like to be the closing speaker at the stadium tribute.

She shook her head and responded, "No, Gill. This morning was about looking back and saying goodbye. Tonight will be dedicated to looking forward and building on his legacy."

Given her feelings, we agreed that the best spot for her to appear on stage at the stadium would be right after Jeff

Stewart was named the new head baseball coach of the Riverview Pioneers.

Although it had seemed like a good idea at the tranquil setting that morning, I wasn't sure how the grieving widow would deal with a huge enthusiastic crowd.

I began my introduction, "Our beloved Coach Mason G. Edwards had the ability to make everyone he encountered feel as though they were the most important person in the world. But right now, I would like to introduce the most important person in his world. Please welcome Margaret Edwards."

The crowd rose as one and applauded as the widow approached the podium. She smiled at me warmly and gave me a quick hug as she whispered, "Thanks, Gill. I couldn't get through all this without you." She seemed confident, but I couldn't help but notice her hands were shaking a bit as she reached out to the podium and looked out over the vast crowd.

She began, "On behalf of my husband and me, I would like to thank you all for being here tonight. When you love someone like I loved Mason, you know that there will be a day when one of you will be alone and grieving. The one left behind will be trying to say goodbye while offering some perspective at a time like this."

She paused, took a ragged breath, and looked out at the loving group of friends, neighbors, and colleagues who had all been greatly impacted by her husband.

She smiled as she seemed to capture a long-ago memory and continued, "I met Mason sixty years ago when we were both students at the teachers' college upstate. I was smitten with him immediately, but he seemed more interested in playing football, basketball, and baseball than he was with me. Little did I know that I would share my life with him, and that would include his love for sports and the young people who play them."

She sighed wistfully and explained, "We were not able to have children, and I feared that it might leave a void in our lives and in our marriage. I didn't realize that in the next half century, we would have thousands of children, and many of you are here tonight as a tribute to his life." A respectful round of applause rose from the stadium. She reached into her pocket, withdrew a piece of paper, unfolded it, and said, "It reminds me of a quote from one of Mason's favorite books: Some people are born into wonderful families. Others have to find or create them. Being a member of a family is a priceless privilege which costs nothing but love."

Margaret Edwards continued to share her memories, "Mason was the smallest, slowest, and weakest player on the football team, the basketball team, and the baseball team." The crowd chuckled. She recalled how she had gone to see Coach Wainwright who coached all three sports at the small college and expressed her concern saying, "Coach Wainwright, I don't think Mason Edwards has the ability to play college sports, and

I'm afraid he's going to die trying." The crowd seemed amused as they were swept up in Margaret's memories.

She recited Coach Wainwright's long-ago response, "Young lady, obviously Mason Edwards means something to you or you wouldn't be here. What you need to understand about players like him is the fact that he won't die trying, but he may die if he doesn't try." Margaret smiled and wiped away a tear, then remembered, "Well, he made the varsity teams in football, basketball, and baseball. He always seemed to be in the most unlikely position where he was physically overpowered but mentally up to the task. On the football team, he would run down on the kickoffs racing past or over several blockers and, more times than not, he would be the first one there to tackle the player returning the kickoff.

"On the basketball team, Mason was known as the hatchet man. They would actually call on him to go into games and foul the opponent's biggest player. On the baseball team, he led the entire league in getting on base by being hit by a pitch. He simply wouldn't move out of the way and was always willing to exchange some bumps and bruises for the chance to be on first base." The crowd applauded knowingly as the widow's story seemed to capture the essence of who they knew Coach Edwards to be.

Margaret resumed her memories, "We got married right after we both finished college. Mason had several offers to be an assistant high school coach somewhere, but when he heard that Riverview was looking for someone to coach football, basketball, and baseball for a meager salary, he leapt on the opportunity." The crowd laughed and Margaret echoed her husband's words, "Margaret, this is a perfect opportunity. The salary is so low that they can't get anyone but me, and I'm going to show them that today will prove to be the luckiest day of their lives."

Margaret beamed with pride as the crowd cheered. She said, "Most coach's wives enjoy the season but look forward to the off season when things slow down a little, and they can enjoy some family time. Well, for more than fifty years, we never really had an off-season. And because Mason's teams got into the playoffs so many times, the seasons actually overlapped one another. He thought it was perfect, and I have to admit, he was right. Mason got many offers to coach at bigger high schools, and even colleges, but he always knew he was in the right place."

The crowd cheered as Margaret turned slightly toward an image that was projected onto the giant screens behind the stage.

She continued, "In Mason's office at home, he hung a poster on the wall next to his desk. It lists several dozen attributes of success, but as you can see, the number one attribute of success is to marry the right person. Well, I know I did, and I believe he did, too." The Riverview fans, friends, and neighbors applauded warmly.

Margaret concluded, "I want to thank each and every one of you for making my Mason's life better and, therefore, for making my life better. You will never know how many hours and days he spent thinking about you all and praying for you. His thoughts and prayers had very little to do with your performance at a practice or in a game, but Coach Edwards wanted you all to find joy and success in your lives. So, when you think about my husband or me, don't feel sorrow. Instead, feel the sense of excitement and expectation he had for each and every one of you. Anytime you are tempted to do anything less than your best, remember Coach Mason G. Edwards and what he taught you through his words and actions."

Loud cheers accompanied a standing ovation as Margaret stepped away from the podium. I hugged her and thanked her for her memories and her message. I told her I was very proud of her but, more importantly, I knew Coach was proud of her. I said, "Margaret, I know that wasn't easy, but as he always said, nothing worth doing is ever easy."

13

Winning Through Giving

"The most rewarding thing you can do with your time, effort, or money is give it away."
—Coach Mason G. Edwards

I accompanied Margaret Edwards back to her seat at the edge of the stage. I thought I might be able to support and assist her, but I think she actually helped me. As she took her seat, I spotted the next speaker I was to introduce. I asked, "Are you ready for this?" The response was just a broad smile and thumbs up.

I smiled as I stood at the podium preparing to introduce the next speaker to give their tribute to Coach Edwards. Augustus Maxwell had been a friend, confidante, and colleague for most of my adult life. He and I began working at Riverview High School the same year, and he had retired just two years before. I began, "Augustus Maxwell, or Gus to all of us who know and love him..." Spontaneous applause erupted from the crowd and chants of "Gus! Gus! Gus!" could be heard echoing throughout the stadium. When the excitement died down, I continued, "Gus served Riverview High School, and everyone who studied and worked here, for almost five decades.

"When he began, he was known as the janitor, then he was called our custodian until he became known as our maintenance engineer, and he retired with the title of Facilities Director. But Gus never altered what he did or changed his job. He always took care of everyone and everything here at Riverview High School. We take a lot of pride in our high school here at Riverview, and we have a lot to be proud of and be thankful for because of people like Gus Maxwell."

Gus strode across the stage smiling from ear to ear. He was an energetic, vigorous African American gentleman in his mid-70s who managed to exude pride and humility at the same time. We shook hands warmly, and Gus stepped to the podium. He gazed slowly across the vast crowd gathered in the football stadium and began.

"I am very proud and pleased to be here tonight to speak about the life and legacy of my friend and mentor Coach Mason G. Edwards. Coach got hired to head up our football, basketball, and baseball programs shortly after I started working for the high school. The first time I met him was when I got called to his office early one morning just after school started that year." Gus told of rushing into Coach Edwards' office and introducing himself. He explained, "The Coach told me that several players had left towels, tape, and some other trash on the floor. When I jumped up to run into the locker room to take care of it, Coach Edwards motioned for me to sit back down."

Gus shared his memories as he recited the coach's long-ago words. "Gus, you and I need to establish our game plan right now. It's your job to take care of the facilities and maintain everything so we can have a first-class operation, but it's my players' responsibility to pick up their towels, take care of their equipment, and clean up their trash. The reason I called you in today was to let you know that I never want you to pick up after my ballplayers or do anything that they are supposed to do themselves. That would rob them of the opportunity to learn discipline, pride, and consistency."

Many people in the crowd could be seen nodding their heads as they remembered Coach's rules. Gus continued, "Coach also wanted me to know that we were going to treat our visiting opponents as we would like them to treat us. He explained that he expected the visitors' locker room and facilities to be impeccable before the opposing teams arrived. Regardless of what other teams did when they came to Riverview, we would never leave a mess in someone else's locker room when we were the visitors. Coach told me that the way players dress and act reflects how they feel about themselves—and the way we take care of our facilities and equipment reflects how we all feel about the team. It's a matter of mutual respect."

Applause could be heard showing approval for the coach's words. Gus sighed thoughtfully and continued, "My entire working life, I had the kind of job that a lot of people look down on or don't think about at all until something needs cleaning or fixing. But Coach Mason G. Edwards made me feel like I was an important part of the team, and I will never forget him for showing me that courtesy and challenging me to rise to a higher standard."

The crowd reacted with applause and cheers for both Coach Edwards and Gus. Gus continued, "It was a great working relationship, and we settled into a consistent pattern just as Coach Edwards had laid it out.

"Everything changed when my oldest boy, Gus Junior, made the varsity basketball team. I was very proud of my son and began to appreciate the coach even more. Junior became a starter just before his senior year, and we were looking forward to great things from him as a basketball player until one night when he just collapsed running down the floor."

Everyone could see that the memory of that long-ago experience with Gus's son still weighed heavily on him. He spoke, "The coach and the doctor rushed out onto the floor to check on my boy, and they called for the ambulance. I walked beside the gurney and climbed into the back of the ambulance after they loaded Junior. Just before they closed the door, Coach Edwards jumped in the back with me. When I asked him about the team and the game, he simply let me know that the assistant coach would handle it, and this was more important. Coach Edwards stayed up with me all night at the hospital and was there when the doctor told us my boy had a serious heart condition that would likely require a transplant."

Gus wiped a tear from his eye and composed himself as he explained, "The doctor here in Riverview told Mrs. Maxwell and me that the best place to have a heart transplant done was in Houston, but we knew there was no way we could make that happen. Coach Edwards, smiled, hugged us both, told us to take care of Junior, and he would take care of everything else.

"Coach told about how one of his former players, an all-state linebacker, had become one of the top heart surgeons in the country and was working out of the best hospital in Houston. The coach had made all the arrangements, the procedure went well, and Gus Junior was given the gift of resuming a normal life." The crowd applauded warmly.

Gus spoke with great emotion, "When someone does something for you, you appreciate it and tell them thank you, but when someone does something for your child, you are grateful but never quite have the right words to say. So, as I stand here tonight paying tribute to my colleague, my friend, and the best man I ever knew, I want you to understand that all my best words times a thousand can't touch what Coach Mason G. Edwards meant to me and my family." The crowd applauded, sharing in Gus's gratitude for Coach Edwards.

Gus remembered, "When I retired a couple of years ago, my wife, Miss Sally, threw a little party for me at the house. There were just a few friends and family members, and we were all shocked when Coach Edwards and Margaret arrived and joined in the celebration. After the party, I walked out onto the porch with Coach and told him I appreciated him coming to the party and how grateful we all were for everything he had done for us."

Gus tried to control his emotions and then he shared with everyone in the Riverview football stadium the Coach's parting words on the porch that evening. Coach Edwards had said, "Gus, the greatest thing that can ever happen to us is not receiving something or having someone do something for us.

It's the privilege of being able to do something for someone you love. So, I will always be grateful to you, Gus Junior, and your whole family for allowing me to be part of your happy ending." The crowd applauded wildly the coach's powerful message that Gus had shared.

When the stadium fell silent once again, Gus announced, "In keeping with Coach's words, deeds, and example, I believe the greatest tribute we can give to him tonight and going forward is to do something for someone else." Gus reached into the pocket of his suit jacket and withdrew a light blue card that he held aloft. He explained, "This is an organ donor card in memory of Coach Mason G. Edwards. Ushers will be passing these out to everyone here tonight, and you can fill them out and drop them off at the tables located at each of the exits as you leave the stadium."

Gus glanced at me and Margaret Edwards sitting behind him on stage and concluded, "I want to thank Mr. Lucas for allowing me to speak tonight, and I want to thank Mrs. Edwards for allowing us all to give this vital gift as our tribute to the late, great Coach Mason G. Edwards."

There was a thunderous standing ovation. Gus waved and held the donor card aloft again as he walked over to where Margaret Edwards and I were standing and applauding. He hugged us both and left the stage.

Later that night, I received a report on the donor cards, and it seemed that everyone who had been in the Riverview

Pioneers football stadium that night had pledged to give the gift of life to someone in the future as a living tribute to their beloved Coach Mason G. Edwards.

14

Winning Through Understanding

"Virtually all questions and conflicts relating to the human condition can be resolved through the Golden Rule."
—Coach Mason G. Edwards

The next speaker who wanted to offer a tribute to Coach Edwards was like the proverbial stranger in a strange land. Coach Bill Radford had been a fixture at Lakeside High School for decades. To say that Riverview High and Lakeside were rivals would be an understatement. I had asked our mascots Mr. and Mrs. Pioneer, who were dressed in traditional garb from the 1850s, to accompany Coach Radford onto the stage. As the trio approached, I began the introduction.

"It's not unusual for family members, friends, colleagues, or teammates to want to express their love and respect at a time like this, but when a fierce rival wants to speak, it means a lot. Ladies and gentlemen, please welcome Lakeside High School Head Football Coach Bill Radford." There was a brief hesitation throughout the stadium as everyone was caught off guard as Coach Radford reached the podium. A polite round of applause could be heard, then the rival coach spoke.

"Well, folks, I have to admit, I never expected to be here speaking to you, and I'm sure you never expected to be sitting out there listening to me." Good natured laughter erupted from the crowd. Coach Radford smiled and resumed, "Coach Edwards and I were fierce rivals many nights in this very stadium, but when the final whistle blew, we always shook hands and remained great friends and respected colleagues. You come to know someone in a very special way when you compete against them. All of you here likely never knew another coach at Riverview other than Mason Edwards, so his performance, philosophy, and attitude seem normal to you. But I can assure you, your coach was one in a million. He regularly did things I never saw any other coach do before or since.

"I remember one night on this very field when Riverview was the defending state champion, and we came over to play you guys. From what I could tell, none of the players from the state championship team had graduated because when Coach Edwards ran onto the field with the team, it looked like the same group from the state championship." The crowd laughed and cheered.

Coach Radford continued, "Our team gave its best effort and exceeded expectations that night, but we got beat by three points. As I was in the visitors' locker room right over there..." He pointed to his left at the tunnel entrance to the locker room, and resumed, "I was trying to console our team when there was a knock on the locker room door. I was very frustrated at being interrupted, so I flung the door open prepared to confront someone, when, to my shock, I saw Coach Edwards standing there. I guess he responded to the shocked and bewildered look on my face and explained that he wanted to talk to my team if that was alright."

Coach Radford paused thoughtfully, and said, "Folks, as I told you, Mason was one in a million. I've never met an opposing coach that I would allow to speak to my team after a game, but I waved him in and told my guys to pay attention."

Bill Radford recalled Coach Edwards' words shared that night. "Gentleman, I want to congratulate each and every one of you on a game well-played. You played much better than my team, and I will be speaking to them about that a little later. But right now, I want you to know regardless of what the scoreboard reads, you are winners. If you'll play every game for the rest of the season and perform every task for the rest of your life with the heart and energy you showed tonight, you will always be successful."

The crowd applauded, Coach Radford smiled and quipped, "What are you gonna do with a guy like that? He beats you in a game, then makes you love and respect him even more." The crowd chuckled and nodded in understanding. Coach Radford resumed, "Now don't kid yourself, Coach Edwards would do anything legal, moral, and ethical to win, and he gave his players every possible advantage. I learned early on to never say anything in public to the media that I didn't want Coach Edwards to get a hold of. I remember telling an eager reporter that I thought Lakeside had a better team than Riverview, and if we played up to our potential, we would undoubtedly win. Coach Edwards took the quote out of the Lakeside newspaper, blew it up to headline size, and posted it throughout the Riverview locker room all week. By game time, your boys were so motivated, we never had a chance." The Riverview crowd cheered for Coach Edwards and the long-ago victory.

Coach Radford told of how he and Coach Edwards had become friends and colleagues in the midst of being rivals. They would often travel together and were roommates at coaches' conventions across the country. Coach Radford recalled, "I remember Mason teaching a group of head coaches at a convention how he graded game film and gave his players feedback. One of the other coaches commented on how Coach Edwards always praised the blockers while having very limited comments about the running backs, receivers, or quarterbacks that scored the touchdowns. Coach Edwards explained to us all that the players scoring touchdowns would get plenty of praise and attention, but the blockers, who really made it possible, could be overlooked unless he, as their coach, praised them."

Coach Radford paused poignantly, appeared thoughtful, then spoke from his heart. "You learn a lot about a friend or a rival in the midst of a crisis. You never really know what's inside of someone until they're under pressure, and then it comes out. Every coach has had players who talked a good game and maybe even practiced well, but when it came down to game time, they couldn't get it done.

"On the other hand, we've all known of players who seemed quiet, small, slow, and weak, but when the lights came on at game time, competition revealed strength, tenacity, and a winning nature that wasn't previously apparent."

Coach Radford collected his thoughts and memories as he continued. "I remember a game on this very field close to thirty years ago. I was a new coach and had just met Mason Edwards that night. Of course, I knew him by reputation even then. In the middle of the second half, one of my players went down with a broken leg. It was a compound fracture, so I knew it was really bad and could create serious complications. He was rushed to your local hospital here in Riverview, and I got there as quickly as I could, but I couldn't beat Coach Edwards. He was already sitting with my player in the emergency room before they took him in to be operated on."

Coach Radford described how, the minute he arrived, Coach Edwards got up and let his rival sit and talk with his player. Coach Edwards asked, "Bill, what can I do for you right now?"

Coach Radford said, "I told him I would be staying here in Riverview for a couple of days to be with my player, so if he could make arrangements for a hotel room and a rental car, it would really help."

Coach Radford sighed with deep emotion as he remembered the scene decades before. He looked at the crowd and explained, "Folks, after my player got out of surgery and they had him settled in a room, I stepped out into the hall and there was Coach Edwards waiting for me. I asked him about my room and car, and he just motioned that I should follow him. We got into his car for what I thought was a ride to a local hotel, but we ended up at Coach Edwards' house. I asked him about the room and car, and he just chuckled and assured me I would have the best room in town, and Margaret's food was the best in the state."

The crowd nodded and smiled as Coach Radford continued. "Well, Coach Edwards was right. They were wonderful hosts, and Margaret's food was some of the best I ever had. Coach Edwards let me use his car and went with me to the hospital every day. When I think back all those years to that time, I really can't remember who won the football game, but I feel like I won one of the greatest friends, colleagues, and mentors any young coach ever had."

The crowd applauded. Coach Radford smiled broadly and concluded, "I want to thank everyone here for giving me the opportunity to say a few words about a great coach and a great man. I will be back here in this stadium this fall on the sideline with my Lakeside football team. We will do our best to win the game, but we will have the victory regardless of the final score because I will share the wisdom and values that Coach Edwards taught me with each of my players. When you live that way, you will always be a winner in the game of life."

15

Winning Through Priorities

"Excellence is only required at a few critical moments. Unfortunately, we never know when they're coming."
—Coach Mason G. Edwards

I shook hands with Coach Radford as he left the stage, and I told him that I hoped he and his team would have great success in the coming season with the exception of the football game here in Riverview. We both laughed good-naturedly, and I turned my attention to the task of introducing Father Patrick O'Neil. I only knew him casually at that time, but I had been at the graveside service he conducted earlier that day, so I knew him to be a spiritual leader with great compassion, wisdom, and grace.

I looked out at the vast crowd as I spoke, "Coach Edwards always reminded me and everyone involved with sports teams here at Riverview High School, that our players are a combination of mind, body, and spirit. This morning, I stood at Coach Edwards' graveside at the Riverview Cemetery and was both comforted and encouraged by the words of Father Patrick O'Neil. Please welcome him to share a few thoughts at this time."

Father O'Neil approached the podium wearing his formal robe and clerical collar. He bowed his head for a moment, smiled warmly, and shared his thoughts. "Ladies and gentlemen, we are gathered here on this solemn but hopeful occasion to celebrate the life well-lived of a beloved man, friend, neighbor, and coach." The crowd applauded respectfully.

Father O'Neil nodded and continued. "I have ministered here in Riverview for fifteen years, and this was my first assignment when I graduated from seminary. When I inquired about the church and congregation I would be leading, everyone told me about Coach Mason G. Edwards as a mainstay in the church as well as a pillar in the community and an iconic figure. I was eager and a bit intimidated to meet this illustrious man everyone had described to me.

"During one of my first services, I encountered one of the deacons in the foyer outside the sanctuary, and I asked him about scheduling some church activities in the coming weeks and months. He pointed up to the ceiling to let me know that I would need to check with the man upstairs." Father O'Neil paused for effect, then admitted, "I thought my deacon was suggesting I seek heavenly counsel or spiritual guidance before finalizing the church schedule. Little did I know, he was referring to Coach Mason G. Edwards who always sat in the balcony for the early service." The crowd laughed.

Father O'Neil smiled and continued, "So I actually got to meet the man upstairs later that morning, and my life as a pastor and a man was forever changed. Coach Edwards was one of those especial souls who touched everyone around him and made them better. Today, as we laid him to rest at the cemetery, I assured everyone that, in the midst of our sadness, we could celebrate a life well-lived and a race fully run."

Everyone in the stadium was struck by the emotional words and powerful thoughts. Father O'Neil explained, "Coach Edwards was much more than a member of my clergy or a prominent figure in our town. He was a mentor and an example to me, but, more importantly, he was my friend." Father O'Neil reached into his pocket and slipped out a greeting card. He held it up for the crowd to see and said, "This is a Christmas card I often carry with me. I received it many years ago from Coach Edwards. I would like to read it to you."

Father O'Neil opened the card and read, "No man is truly poor if he has one friend." He paused and the crowd applauded. He explained that Coach Edwards told him the phrase had been written in a short story that had been shared by an obscure author with a few friends over a holiday season during the Great Depression. One of the copies eventually ended up in the hands of Frank Capra, the movie producer, who turned it into the classic film, *It's a Wonderful Life*.

Father O'Neil said, "As many of you know, our church presents *It's a Wonderful Life* every year as our Christmas gift to the community. Every year since we began the tradition, Coach Edwards would introduce the film by explaining how big things can come from little ideas." Father O'Neil appeared emotional, hesitated for a moment, then continued, "We hope many of you will join us this year for the inspiring presentation of *It's a Wonderful Life* as an ongoing tribute to Coach Edwards because his words have proven true to me and everyone one who knew him. Regardless of our financial status we are all richer because we knew and loved Coach Mason G. Edwards." The crowd applauded enthusiastically.

Father Patrick O'Neil smiled broadly and spoke, "When I meet people for the first time and let them know I'm a pastor, they often want to know how I get the ideas for my sermons each week. Well, throughout my career thus far, I've had a secret treasure chest of inspiring thoughts that all came from my beloved friend Mason Edwards. The greatest piece of advice he ever gave me was the simple idea that before we undertake any task or encounter any situation, we should ask ourselves one simple question." Father O'Neil paused for effect, then spoke the powerful question, "What would I do right now if I were amazing?" Many in the crowd nodded and smiled as they had heard that phrase countless times from Coach Edwards.

Father O'Neil continued, "That question can serve us every day for the rest of our lives and can remind us that there are no insignificant people; there are no insignificant days; and there are no insignificant moments. Everything we do and every person we encounter gives us the opportunity to make a true and lasting difference in the world." The crowd applauded enthusiastically.

Father O'Neil resumed his remarks, "Mason felt that the coaching profession was a significant opportunity to teach and mold young people. He was a man of great thoughts and great ideas. He was well-read and always sought new opportunities to learn and grow. It bothered him that words are the only vehicles we have to share our motivation and inspiration with those around us. He lamented the fact that many of his colleagues in the coaching profession constantly used disrespectful and foul language, and they failed to control their tempers. Coach Edwards told me that, in over fifty years of dealing with young people, he never used bad language, and I've never heard anyone contradict that." The crowd applauded their approval.

Father O'Neil smiled, chuckled, and continued, "Coach Edwards did tell me about a time when one of his basketball teams was several points behind late in an important game. He told me he just couldn't get the young men fired up, so he determined to employ a tactic he occasionally used in such a situation involving getting a technical foul called on himself."

Father O'Neil told how Coach Edwards waited until the right moment, then approached a referee he knew and said, "Frank, I'm in a tough spot here, and I need to get my players fired up, so I want you to give me a technical foul. I know there's a word I can say that will cause you to immediately signal a technical foul on me, but I've committed to not using that kind of language." The crowd cheered their approval and Father O'Neil continued. "Well, apparently, that referee was a man of high standards and deep conviction because he called the foul on Coach Edwards because he knew the word but didn't say it. The players got motivated to rally on behalf of their coach, and Riverview won that game handily." The stadium erupted with applause for the long-ago victory and their beloved Coach Mason G. Edwards.

Father Patrick O'Neil concluded his tribute, "We have all lost a beloved friend and treasured coach, but we haven't lost the inspiration, ideals, and standards he stood for. Mason Edwards wasn't a coach who just prayed before each game. His faith wasn't what he did, it was who he was. In the midst of touchdowns, three-point shots, and homeruns, there was a power and a grace about Coach Edwards that transcended the game and the score. All of us in this place at this time should commit ourselves to taking a piece of Coach Edwards with us, carry it inside of us, and walk it out all the days of our lives."

A standing ovation erupted for the inspiring words and thoughts of Father O'Neil dedicated to his special friend Coach Mason G. Edwards. Father O'Neil bowed his head solemnly, then shook my hand, hugged Margaret Edwards, and took a seat next to her on the stage.

16

Winning Through Planning

"Effort without planning is chaos."
—Coach Mason G. Edwards

I had known Marcus Robbins for many years. Obviously, when I was the athletic director at Riverview High School, I had met him and knew who he was, but he really came to my attention after the horrible accident in which he lost both of his hands. Everyone in our town was aware of him throughout his recovery and admired and respected the way he had adapted to his physical challenges and was living an extraordinary life. He was a prominent and successful entrepreneur with many businesses. He was a loving husband, and a father of three wonderful kids—two of whom were currently students at Riverview High. It's hard to introduce someone who virtually everyone already knows, and since Marty Finn had talked about Marcus earlier in the evening as part of his letterman's jacket incident, I kept it short and sweet.

"Ladies and gentlemen, we all know him, respect him and love him. Please welcome Marcus Robbins." Marcus strode confidently across the stage, and he and I exchanged our customary version of a fist bump that we had developed in the aftermath of his accident. He waved at the crowd with his prosthetic device, which was there in place of a hand, looked out at the vast crowd, and began.

"I want to thank Mrs. Edwards, Gill Lucas, and all of you for giving me the opportunity to speak. I have so much in my life to be grateful for and so many people to thank—first and foremost being Coach Edwards." The crowd cheered and applauded encouraging Marcus as he continued. "As many of you know I was part of Coach Edwards' basketball team until I traded in my hands for these." He held up both of his arms showing his prosthetic hands and continued. "Coach Edwards visited me in the hospital every day and was a constant source of encouragement throughout my recovery and rehabilitation. He never once acted as if he felt sorry for me, and he always expected me to excel and perform at the highest level."

Marcus Robbins paused as the memories of those difficult days flooded over him. He shared, "After I was out of the hospital and the rehab center, Coach Edwards told me he was shifting my position on the basketball team from being a player to being the team manager. I was rather shocked because I didn't know what was involved and he never really asked me as much as he told me. I questioned him as to whether I had any choice in the matter."

Good-natured laughter could be heard from the crowd as everyone anticipated the coach's long-ago reaction. Marcus recited the coach's words, "Robbins, you need to listen to this and remember it. You were, you are, and you will be part of this team. A team stays together and plays together. They win or lose as a unit regardless of what happens to any member of the team. We've got an important role for you, and I'm going to expect you to fill it and fill it well. Is there any part of that you don't understand?"

Marcus Robbins smiled sheepishly, shrugged, and spoke to the audience. "So, what are you going to say to something like that? Thus began my career as the manager of the basketball team, and later that year, I filled the same role for the baseball and football teams."

Marcus Robbins shared from his heart about those dark days after recovery and his concerns as to whether or not he could take care of himself, much less anticipating and fulfilling all the needs of a team. He remembered, "Coach Edwards gave me a crash course on being an outstanding team manager. He told me I would need to always have a master list with me 24 hours a day, 7 days a week. Everything that mattered needed to be on my list, and Coach Edwards emphasized that everything mattered." Marcus reached into the inside pocket of his suit jacket with his prosthetic device and withdrew a small notebook. He explained, "From that moment on and to this very day, I've never been without my master list. It contains all the information for my businesses and my personal life, and I think of Coach Edwards every time I open the cover of this notebook."

Marcus closed the notebook and returned it to his pocket. He then shared some of Coach Edwards' instructions on how to use a master list. "Marcus, it's not only vital to have everything on the list, but you have to double check the list frequently. You have to anticipate everything, and remember that high school athletes are notorious for forgetting everything including their brain. Never assume anything. Anything that's worth doing is worth writing down and worth double checking."

Marcus smiled and gazed at the crowd. They applauded the coach's words and Marcus continued. "Over the years people have asked me how I learned to take care of myself after I lost my hands. I have to tell them that I never thought about taking care of myself because I was always focused on taking care of a whole team. I believe the right answer to any challenge in life is the fact that it isn't about you, and it isn't about me. It's about the people around us that we serve."

The crowd applauded his powerful message as he resumed. "Many of you will remember Coach Edwards was a stickler for reviewing game video. He felt that the secret to winning in the future was to understand the past. He always used a little laser pointer so he could indicate exactly what he wanted his players to see." Marcus Robbins reached into his pants pocket, pulled out a laser pointer, and held it aloft so the audience could see it. Everyone applauded and he admitted, "This laser pointer is a lot like my master list. I don't leave home without it.

"I remember that first year I was the team manager. We went on a road trip, and Coach told me he wanted to review some game film of our opponents before we warmed up for the game. Coach asked me if I had brought his laser pointer. I assured him I had one, reached into my pocket and handed it to him. He stared at me with that Coach Mason G. Edwards patented stare and asked one of his life-changing questions."

The crowd laughed anticipating the Coach's words. "Marcus Robbins, do you mean to stand right there and tell me we are two hundred miles from home, and you, being our team manager, only brought one laser pointer?"

Marcus just nodded his head and remembered Coach Edwards words, "Son, let me explain something to you. When it comes to anything our team needs to be successful, one is none, and two is one. It's like a spare tire for our bus. We have to assume things are going to be lost, stolen, or break down. We can never jeopardize our performance based on things that commonly occur. Do you understand me?"

Marcus stood at the podium and nodded his head vigorously saying, "I told the Coach it would never happen again, and it never did. I didn't feel comfortable on a road trip unless I had at least a dozen laser pointers. Our basketball team actually developed an early form of laser tag to break up the boredom on road trips. I could supply a laser pointer for every member of the team with a couple of spares left over." The crowd laughed, cheered, and applauded their approval.

Marcus Robbins concluded, "Ladies and gentlemen, there isn't anyone in this stadium tonight who couldn't tell similar stories of lessons that Coach Edwards taught them and how it changed them, not only as student athletes here at Riverview High School, but as businesspeople, parents, and successful human beings. You and I now have the responsibility and the privilege of sharing his lessons with our families, friends, colleagues, and everyone we come in contact with. When we receive the blessing that we all have received from the coach, we can do no less than to use it every day and pass it on. He may be gone, but he will never be forgotten. As an ancient wise man said..." Marcus Robbins sighed and ended with those impactful words, "may his shadow never grow less."

The stadium was filled with a resounding ovation. I hugged Marcus Robbins as he walked off stage, and I knew that his words and his example would be a lasting tribute to Coach Edwards and make a difference in all of our lives.

17

Winning Through Leadership

*"If you want to be a leader,
learn how to serve."*
—Coach Mason G. Edwards

The next speaker listed on my agenda for the evening had arrived early and had remained seated on stage behind the podium trying to be respectful and inconspicuous without creating a distraction. But if you're a four-star general and regularly a prominent fixture in the national news, it's hard to go unnoticed. Although he was casually seated in his chair, he seemed to be at attention and fully alert to all going on around him.

I began, "Ladies and gentlemen, it's now my privilege to introduce a man born and raised here in Riverview and a proud graduate of our high school. Please welcome General Franklin J. Potter." The crowd stood and applauded as the general marched to the podium in his dress blue uniform festooned with countless commendations, ribbons, and medals. I shook hands with him even though I felt more like saluting.

He smiled warmly and greeted me saying, "Thank you, sir. It's a privilege to be back in this place even under these circumstances."

The general stood behind the podium at attention until the applause died down, then he began. "Ladies and gentlemen, it's a true honor and privilege to have this opportunity to pay tribute to my mentor and lifelong friend, Coach Mason G. Edwards." The crowd applauded and the general gave a brief nod and continued.

"As I was making way to the stadium this evening, a reporter asked why I had traveled six-thousand miles to be here. I let that reporter know that I had traveled six-thousand miles to be here because that's how far it was from where I'm currently serving in the Middle East to Riverview. If I had been stationed on the dark side of the moon, I would have traveled 240,000 miles to be here." The crowd cheered and applauded. The general explained, "There is no time or distance when it comes to respect, honor, and love. Coach Edwards taught me most of what I know about being a leader.

"I will never forget the first lesson he gave me on the subject. I was hoping to be selected as a captain on the football team my junior year, and I expressed that desire to the coach. He told me the simple truth about being a leader."

The general paused for effect and shared the coach's words. "Frank, a leader is anyone who is worth following." The general paused, nodded his head once as if the matter was fully explained and completely resolved, then continued. "The coach made me aware of the fact that if I wanted to be a leader in the future, I had to start serving others right then. He explained to me that a leader isn't something you're appointed to or given. It's something you earn, and then you are recognized for it."

The general became more conversational as he shared how Coach Edwards' words and example had impacted his life when he was a captain on the football team and now as a general in the army. He recited more of Coach Edwards' wise words. "A leader is a leader all the time. Leaders don't get a day off. And you'll be known for a lifetime of great things you do or one lapse in judgment or character." The crowd applauded Coach Edwards' words.

General Potter continued, "Coach Edwards was an expert in leading teams into competition just as military officers lead men and women into battle. He told me that when the game was on the line, players should not think, they should react. I can assure you that when they are in battle, soldiers should never think. They should always react. To do anything less is to put lives in jeopardy." The crowd cheered the general's powerful words.

He went on to explain that Coach Edwards had taught him that repetition is the mother of skill and allows players or soldiers to react properly instead of hesitating and thinking. "The coach always reminded us that despite the old adage, practice does not make perfect, but instead, practice makes consistent. Therefore, perfect practice makes perfect performances." The general sighed and appeared thoughtful. It was apparent to everyone present why he had become known as one of the world's greatest leaders.

He continued, "I remember a game our senior year when we were behind six points with the clock running out and our opponents had the ball. Coach called time out and motioned me to the sideline because I was the captain on the field. He asked me what I thought we should do, and I shrugged and told him there was nothing we could do because they were going to just run out the clock. Then he gave me one of those stares that demands all your attention and presented me with the wisdom that changed that game, my career, and my life."

The entire stadium was completely silent anticipating the coach's words. "Franklin Potter, we always have a choice. We can always choose to win or lose regardless of our circumstances. Never forget that we always find what we're looking for."

The excitement built as the general shared his memories. "I ran back onto the field and told everyone in the huddle that we were going to get the football, go score, and win this game. Just like I believed the coach, they believed me, and on the very next play, before their quarterback could take the snap and kneel down, our linebacker broke through the line and knocked the ball loose. Then, just as if we'd planned it, our defensive end scooped up the fumble and ran it into the end zone for a touchdown. We kicked the extra point and won the game."

The Riverview crowd cheered the victory, and the general continued, "Ladies and gentlemen, that same principle has played out numerous times in my career in critical life and death situations. If we believe there's a way to victory, and can share that with our team, the thought becomes reality. We do, indeed, change our lives when we change our minds. Coach Mason G. Edwards gave us all a treasured gift when he shared that with his words and actions throughout his entire life."

The general acknowledged the applause and concluded, "As a general, I have the privilege of serving everyone in my command, I have the honor to lead some very special men and women. But I believe Coach Edwards had an even greater calling and mission because he built quality men and women for over half a century. You and I are the living results of all that he did and all that he was." The general sharply stepped back from the podium, turned and saluted the flag at the far end of the field, then crisply marched back to his seat. We all knew that we had heard and seen something very sacred and special that night.

18

Winning Through Consistency

"Turn your best performance into a habit."
—Coach Mason G. Edwards

Pedro Valdez had grown up in a poor and disadvantaged section of San Juan, Puerto Rico. As a child, you could never have convinced him that he wasn't the luckiest kid in the world because he had everything he needed including loving parents and baseball. In Puerto Rico, baseball was a national passion and obsession. It seemed that nowhere on that island nation were you ever more than a few minutes away from a baseball field.

Pedro's idyllic childhood ended that fateful night when he and his parents were in a horrible car wreck after one of his games. Pedro spent several months in a hospital, but his physical scars were nothing compared to the emotional scars he lived with after they told him both of his parents had been killed in the accident.

Once he was able to get around on his own, Pedro went to live with his grandmother in a little town in the United States of America named Riverview. Everything seemed strange, uncomfortable, and out of sorts. He longed for his dusty old neighborhood in San Juan where he could spend every possible minute of every day living out his dreams of playing baseball.

Among the other difficulties Pedro experienced in the tragic life-altering transition, he struggled mightily with speaking English. As a 14-year-old, he was nervous and self-conscious the day he walked into Coach Mason G. Edwards' office. After some halting English and coach's limited Spanish, the two of them connected, and it was understood that Pedro Valdez wanted to be a baseball player at Riverview High School. It was still almost a half-hour before practice was scheduled to start, but several of the pitchers and catchers were already on the field warming up.

Coach Edwards motioned for Pedro to get a bat and show what he could do at the plate. The coach would admit, years later, that he had very low expectations but wanted to give the kid a chance. Pedro was smaller and younger than the other players but, as he stepped into the batter's box, he felt comfortable and at home for the first time since he had left Puerto Rico.

When a great batter hits a baseball, it makes a unique sound instantly recognized by every baseball scout and coach in the world. Coach Edwards was glancing at his roster and going over his notes for that day's practice when he heard that unmistakable sound. He looked up in time to see the ball clearing the centerfield fence with room to spare. The pitcher yelled to the coach, "The kid got lucky, and I'm not really warmed up yet." The coach nodded and motioned for the pitcher to try again.

The second pitch was thrown with more intensity and speed, but the result was the same as the baseball joined its twin somewhere beyond the centerfield fence. After ten more pitches with similar results, Coach Edwards approached Pedro at home plate and asked, "Do you always hit like that?"

Pedro smiled sheepishly and struggled for the words replying, "Pretty normal, I think."

That was the beginning of an amazing baseball season in which the Pioneers' young freshman short stop, Pedro Valdez, became an all-star player and led the team to the playoffs.

Each spring, Coach Edwards did double duty during baseball season and spring football. One day during football practice, the coach noticed Pedro sitting in the stands, and he joined his star shortstop while the football team was running through their warm-up drills. Pedro had seen American football on television, but he had never experienced it in person.

He pointed to the linebackers and told Coach Edwards, "I would like to try that."

Coach Edwards chuckled admiring the young man's spirit but questioning his judgment. He responded, "Son, those are big boys, and they run fast and hit hard. You have a 145-pound body. If you're going to play linebacker, you're going to need a 200-pound attitude."

It turned out that while Pedro did not have the talent or natural aptitude for football that he had for baseball, he made the team and actually got to play a bit his senior year.

One fateful day after baseball practice, Coach Edwards was getting ready to leave and noticed Pedro walking back toward the school building. He followed him and found him in a practice room next to the music class. He was playing an electric guitar. The coach was turning to leave when he stopped in his tracks and just listened to the incredible and inspiring melody drifting down the hall. The next day, when the coach and Pedro were alone, Coach Edwards told Pedro he had heard him playing the day before. Pedro seemed embarrassed and just shrugged.

Coach Edwards asked, "What song was that, and where did you learn to play the guitar?"

Pedro began to speak in Spanish, paused for a moment, then stammered, "It's my song. I learned to play myself."

The Coach admitted, "Pedro, I don't know as much about music as I know about baseball and football, but I would like a couple of friends of mine to hear you play." Pedro was reluctant, but finally agreed.

Coach Edwards and two of his former players met Pedro the following week after practice at his grandmother's home. One of the coach's former players had gone on to become a music producer, while the other was making a living as a studio musician.

Mrs. Valdez welcomed the three men to her small but spotless home. She got them seated in the living room, then went down the hall to Pedro's room. A few moments later, Pedro emerged with a guitar. He plugged it into a small amplifier and just stood there. He seemed impossibly small and young and was scared and intimidated. Finally, the Coach interjected, "Son, you just kick off whenever you're ready." Pedro Valdez seemed to grow in size and in confidence as he placed his hands on the guitar and began to play.

The coach's former players assured Coach Edwards that Pedro was a true prodigy. The coach nodded as their words had confirmed his belief in Pedro's talent.

Later that same evening, Coach Edwards changed the course of Pedro's life when he explained to him and his grandmother, "You have an interest in football, a talent for baseball, and a gift for music. It's great to pursue our interests and enjoy our talents, but all of us go through this life looking for our gift."

Coach Edwards paused, then stared directly into Pedro's eyes declaring, "Son, you've found your gift, and now you have to find the best way you can to give it away to as many people as possible."

Everyone in the Riverview football stadium was reveling in their thoughts and memories of Coach Mason G. Edwards when the stadium lights were dimmed and a spotlight shone on center stage revealing Pedro Valdez standing there holding his now world-famous white electric guitar. In the decades since Pedro had graduated from Riverview High School, he had become a renowned, iconic rock star.

The crowd in the stadium jumped to their feet and were all caught up in a thunderous ovation reminiscent of one of Pedro's outdoor concert venues. Everyone in Riverview had wondered and speculated as to whether Pedro Valdez would come back for Coach Edwards' memorial tribute, but since no one had heard anything about him returning and, since he was in the middle of his world tour, the thought had been dismissed.

The stadium crowd stared in awe at the returning hometown hero. He looked just like he did on television and in his concert movies with one exception. On the body of his guitar, etched in gold, it read, "R.I.P. Coach." As the spotlight beam was refracted into every corner of the stadium, the golden message glowed. No one knew that night that everyone in the world would get to see Pedro Valdez's tribute to Coach Mason G. Edwards because he used that guitar in every concert for the remainder of his world tour.

When the crowd finally fell silent and resumed their seats, Pedro Valdez spoke, "When I first met Coach Edwards, my English wasn't so good." He smiled sheepishly, shrugged and continued, "I think it is still not so great. So, as in many things in my life, I don't speak words, but I let my guitar talk. This is how I will always remember the coach." The rockstar's hands flew over the guitar. The low notes sounded like thunder or the waves of a thousand oceans crashing on a granite shore. The high notes were clear, clean, and piercing, reminiscent of a butterfly soaring up into the clouds.

Everyone who had known Coach Mason G. Edwards used the melody as the soundtrack of the video reel of memories playing in their heads. Pedro Valdez carried everyone away, then brought his musical tribute to a climactic close. As the last note faded into the distance, as if on cue, a shooting star streaked across the sky. The spotlight went out and the stadium lights came on. Pedro Valdez had disappeared. The crowd sat in stunned silence for several moments, then another tumultuous standing ovation erupted.

Many memorable thoughts and words were shared at Coach Mason G. Edwards' stadium tribute, but none of them had any more emotion, intensity, or meaning than the musical tribute offered by the legendary rockstar Pedro Valdez.

19

Winning Through Laughter

"If you can't laugh at yourself, the whole world will be laughing at you."
—Coach Mason G. Edwards

I stood at the podium prepared to introduce the next tribute speaker, but the crowd was still caught up in the excitement and emotion of Pedro Valdez's performance. I thought a bit of levity as a transition might help. I said, "Allow me to reintroduce myself. I am Gill Lucas, Riverview's longtime athletic director and team manager for Coach Edwards." I paused for effect then quipped, "I just wanted to clarify that because a lot people confuse me with Pedro Valdez."

Laughter roared throughout the stadium, and I felt we were all on the same page again. I declared, "I would like to do anything in my life, just one time, as well as Pedro Valdez plays that guitar." The crowd applauded their agreement with my thoughts.

I glanced at my notes and began, "Mr. Myron Speck has been the vice principal here at Riverview for well over thirty years. He asked for the opportunity to share a few of his thoughts and memories tonight. Please welcome him."

A polite smattering of applause could be heard as Mr. Speck approached the podium. I really had no idea what he wanted to talk about and wasn't sure how much of a connection he had with Coach Edwards, but when he asked to speak, Margaret Edwards and I felt it was appropriate to give him the opportunity. He was dressed in his normal nondescript dark suit. He wore horn-rimmed glasses, and his hair always seemed to be just one generation out of style. He gave me a quick, nervous handshake, then adjusted the microphone creating annoying feedback throughout the stadium. He awkwardly stood at the podium and stared down at his hands for an uncomfortable period of time, then slowly spoke.

"You're probably wondering why I'm here. As I stand before you this evening, *I* am wondering why I'm here. Most people matriculate completely through Riverview High School without having much to do with me unless they have some sort of problem." A few nervous chuckles could be heard. Mr. Speck looked up at the crowd creating reflections off his glasses and resumed. "If you follow any of the graffiti that pops up from time to time here at our school, I am known as a geek, a nerd, or several other creative terms unsuitable to mention on this occasion." The crowd applauded politely and seemed to be a bit more comfortable with Mr. Speck but still curious why he was there.

Myron Speck smiled broadly, had a brief moment of silent laughter, then spoke. "Coach Mason G. Edwards was one of my great friends. I did not share his passion for sports, nor did he share my interest in school administration. But we connected deeply and formed a relationship involving humor." Everyone in the stadium seemed shocked and bewildered. Mr. Myron Speck glanced down nervously, sighed as if he were deep in thought, then shared his memories.

"It was thirteen years ago this summer when I was diagnosed with a very serious form of cancer." The crowd fell silent and became very attentive. He continued, "Since it was during the summer recess, none of my colleagues at the school were aware of my condition or the fact that I was in the hospital preparing for surgery. I had never had any interactions with Coach Edwards other than an occasional greeting when we passed in the hall. So you can imagine how shocked I was when he walked into my hospital room as if he were one of my best friends."

The curiosity built throughout the crowd as Myron Speck shared, "Coach Edwards knew about my condition and the upcoming operation. Apparently, one of my doctors had been a basketball player on one of his teams. Coach Edwards was very positive and reassuring throughout his visit, and he left me with a book that he encouraged me to read before my operation, and then he assured me he would be back to check on me."

Mr. Speck shrugged remembering the long-ago encounter, then continued. "The book that Coach Edwards gave to me was entitled, *The Anatomy of an Illness* by Dr. Norman Cousins. It describes Dr. Cousins' research into the positive impact of humor and laughter on illness and recovery. I began reading the book and, if nothing else, it took my mind off the pending procedure right up until the moment they took me to the operating room."

Mr. Speck went on to describe how the surgery had gone pretty much as expected, and after a brief time in post-op, they wheeled him back into his hospital room where Coach

Edwards was waiting. The coach declared, "All is well. The reports are good, and it's time for us to start doing our part in getting you well." Mr. Speck remembered how Coach Edwards then turned on a television and video player he had brought into the hospital room.

Mr. Speck remembered, "Over the next few days, Coach Edwards and I watched an untold number of Marx Brothers movies, Three Stooges videos, and one of his favorite routines which was Abbott and Costello's 'Who's on First.' We laughed until we cried and became great friends. Few people ever knew of our connection, but it was something we shared for the rest of his life, and I will keep with me for the rest of my life."

Myron Speck smiled broadly and seemed to become more comfortable and relatable to the audience who felt as though they were just getting to know him for the first time. He continued, "Apparently, Coach Edwards had learned from the hospital staff that the third day after surgery would be particularly difficult for me, so he slipped into my room while I was sleeping, prepared himself, then waited for me to wake up." Myron Speck actually chuckled and seemed to be filled with anticipation as he declared, "There are some things far better to show you than tell you."

Mr. Speck turned as an image appeared on the giant screens behind the stage. It showed our very own Coach Mason G. Edwards wearing a clown nose, giant wax lips, and a bright orange fright wig. The crowd sat in stunned silence, and then burst into uncontrolled laughter. Just as they all thought they had known Myron Speck to be a soft-spoken, bland administrator, they assumed the coach was a no-nonsense, intense leader. But now, new aspects of both men's personalities were being revealed.

When the crowd fell silent, Mr. Speck spoke briefly of the hidden facets of people that often hold their greatest treasures. He implored everyone to remember that what they observe of another person is not the entire dynamic of that individual. He quoted Mark Twain, "It ain't what you don't know that gets you into trouble. It's what you know for sure that just ain't so."

The crowd applauded warmly and laughed at the irony of Vice Principal Myron Speck discussing humor and quoting Mark Twain.

Mr. Speck concluded, "Ladies and gentlemen, I want to thank Mrs. Edwards and Mr. Lucas for the opportunity to offer a bit of laughter and a humorous tribute to my beloved friend Mason G. Edwards. I want to thank all of you for being here, and I hope you will remember that laughter is the spice of life that improves every situation. And finally, as the scriptures remind us, laughter is, indeed, good medicine." Mr. Speck paused and looked meaningfully at the crowd, then concluded, "And our world is sorely in need of some good medicine."

Vice Principal Myron Speck reached into his suit pocket with all the solemnity that he could muster, took out a party whistle, and blew on it. As the paper streamer unfurled and the sound was amplified throughout the stadium, the crowd roared with laughter. He turned, waved, and walked from the stage.

Vice Principal Speck paused to hug Mrs. Edwards, and then shook my hand and thanked me. But it wasn't like the timid handshake we had exchanged previously. It was warm and vigorous. I knew I would always remember that moment, and I committed to never again assume that what I saw was all there was to any person.

20

Winning Through Gratitude

"The quickest way to get what you want is to be thankful for what you already have."
—Coach Mason G. Edwards

I want to thank Vice Principal Speck for reminding us all to laugh." I once again was addressing the huge crowd in the stadium. "There are times when you either laugh or you cry, and on nights like this, you do both."

I glanced at my notes dealing with my next introduction and began, "I remember James Delroy as a shy, skinny, awkward kid who Coach Edwards built into a great power forward on our basketball team and a dominant tight end who played football in this stadium." The crowd applauded and eagerly anticipated the next speaker. "James Delroy has been called the storyteller of his generation. He is the bestselling author of more than fifty books, and a dozen of his novels have been turned into major motion pictures. Whether you've enjoyed Mr. Delroy's work on the page or on the screen, he has no doubt given us all hours of entertainment and inspiration, so please welcome him."

James Delroy walked across the stage and confidently stood at the podium. The image I had of him as a teenager was long gone, replaced by a confident, creative force and thought leader.

He began, "I want to thank Mr. Lucas for that kind introduction in spite of his accurate description of me as awkward, shy, and skinny. As I stand here today back in in my hometown to try to add some of my own perspective to the life and legacy of Coach Edwards, the only portion of Mr. Lucas's description I continue to strive to embrace is skinny." The crowd applauded and laughed.

James Delroy smiled broadly and continued. "Being a writer is, quite simply, hard work. A great author once described it as opening up a vein and hoping something comes out." James Delroy paused thoughtfully and then shared his memories.

"I am grateful to have known and to have been molded and influenced by Coach Mason G. Edwards. He gave me the framework for living a life of gratitude." James Delroy reached into his pocket, took out a sheet of paper and unfolded it. He explained that during one football season, he was constantly complaining about an ankle injury that just wouldn't heal up, so he was playing with pain each week. The coach told him he could complain all he wanted to once he filled out his Golden List.

Mr. Delroy held up the sheet of paper and declared, "This is today's Golden List. I have had one for every day of my life since Coach Edwards introduced the concept to me when I was seventeen years old." James Delroy explained that when he had asked Coach Edwards about a Golden List, the coach had explained that it was a process he had gotten from his grandmother, and it's simply the act of writing down ten things each day that you are thankful for.

James Delroy looked at the Golden List on the podium before him, then spoke, "Coach told me if I would just fill out my Golden List each day, I would live a great life and forget whatever I was going to start complaining about." The crowd applauded, and he admitted, "I did it for several days after

Coach Edwards told me about it with the goal of proving him wrong. Any of you who ever tried to prove Coach wrong likely found the same result I did." The crowd laughed good-naturedly, and James Delroy began to run through his list.

"Today I am thankful for the chance to be back in my hometown of Riverview. I am thankful for the opportunity to pay my respects to Coach Mason G. Edwards. I am thankful that the coach instilled a love of reading in me that grew into a love for writing." The great author paused, looked up from his Golden List and explained, "One day during basketball practice, Coach Edwards said something about John Steinbeck, probably because he knew I was supposed to be reading Steinbeck's great book, *Travels with Charley: In Search of America* in Mrs. Grimes' English class."

James Delroy paused, shrugged, and smiled sheepishly as he continued, "I believe the operative phrase there would be *supposed to be* reading because I had not touched the book, and I thought John Steinbeck was the forward I would be guarding during the next basketball game." The crowd laughed uproariously, and Delroy continued. "After practice that day, sitting on the bench next to my locker was a copy of *Travels with Charley: In Search of America* by John Steinbeck. There was a note attached to it telling me I should read this book and return it. It was simply signed: Coach."

He remembered the events of that fateful day in his youth and continued. "Well, I read that book and brought it back to coach. He nodded and handed me a copy of *Think and Grow Rich* by Napoleon Hill and instructed me to do it again." The crowd laughed good naturedly as the best-selling author continued, "From that day to this very day, I have never been without one of Coach Edwards' books, and he has always had one from me. For more than three decades, we got into the habit of exchanging books and then discussing them. I can honestly say I would not be who I am today if not for Coach Edwards and his encouragement to become a reader."

James Delroy looked back down at his Golden List and announced, "The fourth thing I'm thankful for tonight is that Coach Edwards taught me that anything you do for twenty-one days becomes a habit. That goes for good habits and bad habits, so I have always endeavored to build my career and my life on good habits.

"The fifth item on my Golden List for which I'm grateful today is that I learned from the coach that everyone has a story, and people love to both hear and tell stories, which became the basis for my life's work.

"The sixth thing on today's Golden List is that the coach taught me principles are encapsulated in great stories." James Delroy looked up at the crowd and spoke to them, "Many of you have no doubt heard on countless occasions during a tough practice or difficult session in the weight room, Coach's story about the tortoise and the hare." The crowd laughed as they all had their own memories of the coach's stories.

James Delroy resumed, "I could stand here for an hour telling you the benefits of hard, diligent work versus being a flash in the pan. Or I can just briefly mention the tortoise and the hare, and you are instantly in tune with that principle."

He looked back down at the list spread out in front of him and read, "The seventh item on my Golden List today is that, thanks to Coach Edwards, I live every day of my life with a morning routine. Like the coach, I like to get up early and get ahead of the whole world. The coach described it as creating success on autopilot." The crowd applauded their approval.

James Delroy smiled and resumed reading from his Golden List. "The eighth thing I'm thankful for today is the fact that Coach taught me I should never put myself in a position to suffer unforced or undisciplined penalties. When I was playing football on this very field, I learned quickly that the coach was quite forgiving if I was called for a penalty during a play. He felt that those penalties involved effort and technique. But any penalties before or after the whistle, like jumping offsides before the snap or getting an unsportsmanlike conduct flag after a play, would put the coach in an extremely disagreeable mood." The crowd laughed knowingly as Delroy continued. "And as you all know, when the coach felt disagreeable, he had a tendency to let you know about it." The laughter roared throughout the stadium.

James Delroy looked back down at his list and said, "The ninth thing I'm thankful for on my Golden List for today is that the coach taught me that words matter. It makes a difference what we think and what we say. Coach Edwards would never talk about the fact that we should not fumble the football. He would instead, simply implore us to hold onto the football. Later in my life, during one of the times we were reviewing a book we had both read, I was complaining about writer's block. Coach assured me I didn't have writer's block. I simply had an inspiration that was building and would reveal itself shortly." The crowd applauded. Many of them had learned similar lessons from coach that they had applied in their own lives.

James Delroy concluded the reading of his Golden List. "The tenth and final item on my Golden List for this very special day is the fact that the coach taught me, in my life and in my business career, that success and money are nothing more than the result of creating value in the lives of other people. So, we should remember that the only people who *make* money work at the US Mint and print dollar bills. The rest of us *earn* money by serving others." The crowd cheered and applauded their approval.

James Delroy continued, "So in the final analysis, as coach taught us all, it's not about me and it's not about you, it's about the people we serve. And no one ever did that better than our beloved Coach Mason G. Edwards."

The crowd rose to their feet and the thunderous ovation could be heard throughout the stadium. James Delroy refolded his Golden List and returned it to his pocket. He smiled broadly, waved to the crowd, and left the stage.

21

Winning Through Legacy

"The most important seeds we plant will bloom long after we're gone."
—Coach Mason G. Edwards

Although I knew the evening was winding down and I only had a few items left on my agenda, I understood they would be impactful, and I hoped and prayed everything would be a worthy tribute to my beloved friend Mason Edwards. I looked at the huge crowd that still seemed attentive and energetic after a long evening, and I began, "I've long believed that one of the greatest privileges in this life is to get to meet and interact with the greatest people of your generation. Well, if you think back on our program this evening, you'll realize we've done just that, greatly due to the influence and example of Coach Edwards. Right now, I would like to introduce a pretty fair defensive end and our United States Senator, the honorable Edmund J. Spears." The crowd rose to their feet and warmly welcomed the senator. He strode purposefully to the podium and smiled warmly as someone accustomed to addressing large crowds.

He began, "Ladies and gentlemen, I want to thank you for that warm welcome. In these days of partisan politics and contentious campaigns, it's wonderful to gather together simply as people from Riverview who loved Coach Edwards." The crowd applauded warmly, and the senator continued. "In the days leading up to this event, I was asked by several members of the media if there were any lessons I had learned from Coach Edwards that helped me in my political career."

The senator paused, nodded vigorously, and proclaimed, "All of us have lessons from the coach that have impacted what we do and who we are. In my public life, coach's admonition to always do what you said you were going to do has been the overarching motivation for everything I pursue in office."

Senator Spears paused collecting this thoughts and memories and shared, "I never doubted the coach would do exactly what he said he would do. He didn't just teach through his words. He taught through his actions. On one particular play during a critical game on this field, I lined up offsides and the referee threw the flag and gave us a five-yard penalty. When I came off the field, the coach was there to greet me."

The crowd laughed in anticipation and the senator continued, "I tried to explain to the coach that my toes had been barely over the line, and he assured me that if I ever again lined up with my toes over the line of scrimmage, he would chop them off." Laugher thundered throughout the stadium, and the senator resumed, "Well, I never doubted that the coach would do exactly what he said he would do, so I never lined up offsides again, and I am pleased to be addressing you tonight with all ten toes intact. Coach Edwards' wisdom served me well on the football field and continues to serve me well on the floor of the United States Senate."

The senator took an envelope out of his pocket, withdrew a single sheet of paper, unfolded it, and explained, "As I was leaving my office in Washington yesterday to travel here, I received this envelope and wanted to share the letter inside it with you all."

He looked down at the page and read, "To all of you gathered in Riverview to pay tribute to a great American, Coach Mason

G. Edwards, Susan and I convey our greetings, condolences, thoughts, and prayers to you all. I never had the privilege of meeting Coach Edwards in person, but I have experienced his influence on numerous occasions. It's much like the fact that, while no one has ever seen the wind, we all have seen the leaves blowing in the trees. Interacting with those who were influenced, formed, and shaped by Coach Edwards is a living lesson in excellence, diligence, and deeply held principles. Although he will not be with you in person, his impact will continue to grow in the hearts and lives of every one of you." The senator paused, looked at the crowd poignantly, then concluded, "And it's signed Gilbert Newman, President of the United States of America."

The crowd applauded wildly and when the stadium fell silent again, the senator continued. "At this time, we have a brief announcement to make, and I would like the director of our state's Department of Education, Mr. Howard Bailey, to join me." The crowd welcomed Mr. Bailey with applause.

He shook hands warmly with the senator, then announced, "Thanks to funding procured by Senator Spears, I am pleased to announce this evening that, throughout the coming summer, this stadium will be undergoing extensive renovations and will reopen in the fall as our state's premiere high school sports venue." The crowd applauded enthusiastically as a rendering of the new stadium appeared on the giant screens above the stage.

The senator stepped to the microphone and proclaimed, "When this stadium reopens as a state-of-the-art football facility, it will be known as the Coach Mason G. Edwards Memorial Stadium." The crowd sprang to their feet and applauded wildly.

I shook hands with the Director of the Department of Education and the senator as they left the stage, then I moved to the podium and announced, "Well, folks, we have one more speaker, but this one requires a bit of a special introduction, so will you please welcome the love of the coach's life, Margaret Edwards, as she joins me here at the podium."

Margaret smiled and waved acknowledging the applause. She hugged me warmly, and I knew she was fighting to contain her emotions. I stepped back and let her address the crowd, "All I can say at this moment is that Mason would be proud and pleased. He hadn't announced it yet, but he was planning to retire this summer. Since his health was declining quickly, and he knew he would be called upon to speak at a retirement banquet, he recorded a video." Margaret smiled knowingly as a single tear slid down her cheek. She stepped back and left the podium to me.

"Folks, we've all heard tonight what some really special people had to say about Coach Edwards. But right now, we're going to close this evening by letting the Coach speak for himself."

The stadium lights dimmed, and Coach Edwards appeared on the giant screens. The effects of his illness were apparent, but the fire in his eyes was undiminished. He spoke, "Ladies and gentlemen, I want to thank you for allowing me to address you in this manner this evening, as I realized, due to my progressing illness, there was no other way I would be able to speak to you.

"When I look back over my life and career, I have many things to be grateful for. I first want to thank my beloved wife, Margaret. Many people have asked me throughout the decades how I could continue to coach multiple sports year-round. Well, I was able to do all that I did because Margaret did everything else. I made a living, but she created a life for us. And no one ever had a better life companion and soulmate.

"I want to thank my beloved friend and colleague Gill Lucas for helping me with every detail from my first day on the job through this moment. When our country was being explored and opened up by those original pioneers who were the inspiration for our team name, they had a phrase they used for someone who was reliable, dependable, and trustworthy. Those pioneers were often in situations where they had no idea what was around the next bend of the river or where the rapids were, so they identified the most special among them as 'a man to ride the river with.' Ladies and gentleman, for more than half a century, Gill Lucas has been a man to ride the river with.

"And now it won't surprise you that I can't conclude my remarks this evening without doing a little bit of coaching." The crowd laughed, but there wasn't a dry eye in the stadium. The coach's voice boomed from the loudspeakers for all to hear.

"Always remember that you have one and only one God-given right and that's the right to choose. You are who you are and where you are in every area of your life because of the choices you've made in the past. If I were to put that another way, all of the choices you've made in your entire life have brought you to this place, at this time, siting right there." The coach paused and pointed toward the camera lens which made every person in the stadium feel as if he were talking to them.

He smiled from the big screens, then continued, "The wonderful thing about understanding this principle is that once you've accepted the responsibility for your past and your present, you will understand that your future will be whatever you want it to be starting tonight. Furthermore, I want you to understand that you are sitting there right now simply one quality decision away from anything you want because *you change your life when you change your mind.* That is the most dynamic concept you will ever encounter. All victory and all success begins with someone willing to change their mind."

The coach paused thoughtfully then concluded, "We all had big dreams when we were teenagers or young adults, but too often the pressures of life set in, and the next thing we know, years or decades have gone by, and our big dream is just buried with our old memories at the bottom of our soul.

"Before you leave this place, I want you to understand that the biggest dream you ever had in your entire life is alive and well, and the only thing you've got to do to activate it in this moment is simply change your mind and say yes to the big dream. Ralph Waldo Emerson reminded us that there's nothing capricious about nature. What that great writer and thought leader meant was that the God who made you and everything you'll ever do, know, and have, would not have put the big dream inside of you if you didn't have the capacity to achieve it. So, ladies and gentlemen, the question is never, can we? The question is always, will we? And your future awaits."

The coach nodded, smiled warmly and his recorded image froze on the giant screens.

The stadium fell silent as everyone was caught up in the emotion of the coach's words, their memories of him, and their big dreams for the future.

A full moon hung over the stadium, and thousands of stars decorated the night sky. We all knew we had been somehow changed and transformed by the power and presence of our beloved Coach Mason G. Edwards.

About Jim Stovall

In spite of blindness, Jim Stovall has been a National Olympic weightlifting champion, a successful investment broker, the president of the Emmy Award-winning Narrative Television Network, and a highly sought-after author and platform speaker. He is the author of more than 50 books, including the bestseller, *The Ultimate Gift*, which is a major motion picture from 20th Century Fox starring James Garner and Abigail Breslin. Eight of his other novels have also been made into movies with two more in production.

Steve Forbes, president and CEO of *Forbes* magazine, says, "Jim Stovall is one of the most extraordinary men of our era."

For his work in making television accessible to our nation's 13 million blind and visually impaired people, The President's Committee on Equal Opportunity selected Jim Stovall as the Entrepreneur of the Year. Jim Stovall has been featured in the *Wall Street Journal, Forbes* magazine, *USA Today*, and has been seen on Good Morning America, CNN, and CBS Evening

News. He was also chosen as the International Humanitarian of the Year, joining Jimmy Carter, Nancy Reagan, and Mother Teresa as recipients of this honor.

THANK YOU FOR READING THIS BOOK!

If you found any of the information helpful, please take a few minutes and leave a review on the bookselling platform of your choice.

BONUS GIFT!

Don't forget to sign up to try our newsletter and grab your free personal development ebook here:

soundwisdom.com/classics